Allison Wo

BOAR HELL

Appalachian
Vengeance

A Backwoods Horror Tale

OVK Publishing House

CONTENT

Chapter 1:

Where the Road Ends

The pickup truck rumbled along the narrowing mountain road, its tires crackling over gravel and the crisp remains of last autumn's needles. Pines leaned in from both sides like silent sentinels—tall, ancient, unmoving—their black-green silhouettes carved hard into the dimming afternoon sky. The windshield was streaked with dried mud and fresh mist. Somewhere behind the clouds, the sun was retreating, indifferent.

The forest rose like a dark tide on either side of the road. It didn't just surround them—it enclosed. Towering trunks pressed in with quiet purpose, their limbs netting the fading light. The kind of wilderness that felt… aware. There was a stillness here, deep and old, like the trees were listening, weighing every word spoken in their shadow. Some thin mist hung low over the ditch line, not yet fog, but enough to soften the edges of the world—like the forest was keeping its secrets close, and had no intention of revealing them to just anyone.

Inside the cab, the air was close. Not just from the heat trapped under layers of flannel and canvas, or the stale tang of gasoline and cigarette smoke. There was something heavier—an unspoken weight riding shotgun. The kind of silence that meant too much had already been said.

Nate sat in the backseat, cramped between a dented cooler and a steel rifle case that rattled with every turn. He hadn't said much since they left the gas station. Just leaned against the cold window, arms crossed loosely, his gaze drifting not toward the road ahead, but sideways—into the blur of trees, as if trying to look past the bark and shadow, into something deeper. Something buried.

Tall and lean, somewhere in his early thirties, Nate looked like a man misfiled by the wilderness. His hair was combed too neatly for mountain air, the kind of order that didn't last long out here. The cuffs of his jeans were still clean, unbrushed by mud or bark, and the jacket he wore—brand new, store-bought for the occasion—hung stiff on his frame, its creases too sharp, its fabric too untouched by rain or blood. He looked prepared in all the wrong ways. There was a narrowness to him, not just in frame but in presence, like a man who'd taught himself to take up less space. The kind of quiet that came from years of swallowing things whole. His eyes—grayish, like weathered glass—moved but rarely settled. Listening more than speaking. Watching more than reacting. A man who had spent most of his life on the outside of circles like this one, and had long since stopped pretending he belonged.

The others filled the space around him. Their voices were louder than the engine. Laughter, sarcasm, stories sharpened by memory and moonshine. They talked over each other, jabbing elbows, cursing the road, debating calibers and terrain. But more than anything—they laughed. It filled the cab like smoke, clinging to the roof, to the corners, to the back of Nate's throat. And with each mile, each snort and shout, the walls seemed to press tighter around him.

«Hey, Nate!» Tyler called from the passenger seat, without turning. His voice had that lazy curl to it, a drawl dipped in amusement and something colder beneath. «You bring bug spray, or you want us to swat the flies off your ass all weekend?»

Laughter burst across the cab—raw, metallic. The kind of laugh that doesn't need a punchline, just a target. It bounced off the windows and rolled down Nate's spine. He didn't smile. Just blinked slowly and turned his head slightly, not enough to meet Tyler's eyes, but enough to let the joke pass through him like smoke through mesh.

«Yeah... hilarious,» he said, voice flat. «Still killing it after the hundredth time. Gets better every damn time, doesn't it?»

From the front seat, Tyler chuckled, slow and dry, like boots dragging through dry leaves. He turned halfway around, elbow hooked over the backrest, bracelets clinking — leather thongs, rusted charms, bits of bone or stone that looked carved by hand. They swayed with every bump in the road, catching Nate's eye for a moment like hypnotic pendulums.

Tyler looked like someone who hadn't quite decided whether to become a myth himself — tall, wiry, half-shadowed by a trucker cap pulled low. His one visible eye, the left, was pale blue, sharp as chipped ice. The other was milky, glazed — blind, or something worse. His grin was crooked, stained by tobacco, and it twisted wider now like a knife wound stretching open.

«I'm not laughing at you, man. Every group needs a vegan,» Tyler said, mock-serious, his grin twitching at the corners like he was holding in something darker. «It's, like, tradition.»

A burst of laughter followed, loud and sharp, bouncing off the truck's ceiling like loose bolts in a tin. Someone in the back let out a wheezing snort. Another slapped the dash with too much amusement.

Nate didn't move.

He let out a slow, nasal exhale — not quite a sigh, not quite a snort — and shifted slightly in his seat. His eyes stayed on the trees outside, watching the blur of pine trunks and shadows pass like ghosts. His lips tightened, jaw set. Not in anger. Not yet. But it was wearing thin. All of it. The jokes. The jabs. The sense that he was being weighed, measured, and coming up short— again.

The forest looked better than these people. At least the forest didn't talk.

Then Tyler shifted forward slightly. His voice lost the mocking edge, turned quieter — almost thoughtful.

«I'm serious, though. How's city life treating you? Still got that job in the suit-and-tie world? Offices, screens, traffic lights… All that shit?» He nodded out the window, where the trees grew thicker and darker. "Then bam — here we are. Middle of nowhere. Just you, and the dirt, and whatever's out there."

He paused, smirked again.

"You nervous, Nate?"

There was a beat of silence.

«Not really,» came the flat reply.

A few chuckles rippled in the cab, like water skipping off dirty glass.

Even Jesse — the one behind the wheel — allowed himself a faint smirk. It didn't reach his eyes.

Nate noticed. He always noticed.

Jesse looked like him — same jawline, same brow, like two versions of the same photo separated by time.

But where Nate wore tension like a too-tight shirt, Jesse carried himself with the weary calm of someone who'd long since accepted the forest's silence.

They hadn't said they were brothers.

They didn't need to.

Anyone who saw them, even once, just knew.

The air in the cab shifted again — colder, tighter — when the voice from the passenger side cut in.

"Alright, that's enough," came a sneer from Rayan beside the window. His head was shaved down to a buzz, his face all angles and shadow, like it had been carved from gristle. A scar traced from his temple down behind his ear, and his eyes — small, sharp, full of static — pinned Nate like crosshairs.

"We're not out here to make s'mores," he said, grinning with teeth too white for his personality.

The others laughed again. Quieter this time.

"When was the last time you held a rifle that wasn't in a video game?"

His voice was like a snapped wire — thin, high, and sharp enough to cut. Every word carried that metallic whine, as if underneath it all was the buzz of something broken and mean.

Nate looked at him. Just for a second.

Then leaned back against the cool glass of the window and said, dryly:

«You guys not sick of this yet?»

Rayan grinned wide, clearly pleased with himself.

He had caught the reaction — the flicker of Nate's jaw tightening, the way his shoulders pulled in a little. He saw it, and leaned into it.

"Hey, relax, man. We're just messing with you," he said, still smiling, but there was something sour behind it. A hint of teeth. "Didn't know you were so touchy."

Nate turned back to the window without answering, trying to lock his eyes on something — anything — far off in the trees. A trunk, a shadow, a line of moss on bark. Something real. Something solid. Something that didn't talk.

From behind, another voice chimed in, light and stupid.

"Y'know," said Dale, sitting in the middle seat, twisting toward the front, "they say you're not supposed to go into the woods when you're all riled up. Wild animals can sense that kinda thing. Like dogs, man. They smell it on you."

His face twisted into a cartoonish snarl, as if mimicking a bear or wolf — though he looked more like a kid trying to scare his reflection in the mirror.

He was broad, soft around the middle, his T-shirt stretched tight across his gut. Cheeks puffed and pink, always jiggling slightly whenever he spoke or laughed — which was often. His laughter had that high, wheezy pitch that always came too loud and too long, cutting through every conversation whether invited or not.

"Seriously," he went on, giggling, "you go stompin' into the woods all angry and annoyed? Boom. Something catches your scent and — bam! You're lunch."

He laughed again, his whole body bouncing with it, then reached over and gave Nate a friendly slap on the shoulder — too hard, too familiar.

Nate flinched slightly, let out a short exhale through his nose, somewhere between a laugh and a warning.

His lips pressed tight. Not angry. Just... tired.

"I just don't get why I'm the damn center of attention the whole ride," he muttered.

From the driver's seat came a softer voice — lower, steadier.

"'Cause everybody missed you," Jesse said with a small, lopsided smile.

And for the first time, Nate didn't feel like snapping.

That smile — quiet, without mockery — was the only one in the truck that didn't make his skin crawl.

"We're almost there," Jesse added, a little louder.

Nate gave a faint smile of his own, barely more than a twitch at the corner of his mouth. He turned his head again, watching the blur outside.

Trees passed in smudges of green and brown. Ferns fanned out at the roadside, their bright leaves catching light like little flags. Moss crawled up the trunks, dense and velvet-rich. The Appalachian woods were growing deeper, thicker — not just forest, but place. Old. Breathing.

Somewhere near the front, the bracelets on Tyler's wrist clinked again — bone, twine, metal — a soft jingle like windchimes made from old teeth.

The truck suddenly jolted — hit a root or something worse.

The cooler beside Nate jumped an inch, and the rifle case shifted with a metallic clatter, bumping hard against his thigh.

He looked down at it.

Then nudged it back with a single finger — not violently, not disgusted — but like he wanted to be sure it wasn't touching him.

Not more than it had to, anyway.

The voices around him kept humming in their own uneven rhythm, rising now and then into laughter, dropping back into muttered jokes and elbow nudges. Nate wasn't really listening anymore. He was there—physically, anyway—but something about being packed into this truck with these men was stirring something inside him.

Something old.

Something that had been buried deep, shoved down hard and left for dead.

And now it was crawling back up.

He wasn't ready for it.

He looked out at the forest as it thickened. The trees were older here, bark curling like burned paper, branches reaching like claws. Undergrowth clung tight to the earth. The road was narrowing, the ruts deeper, the light dimmer. It didn't feel like they were driving into wilderness.

It felt like they were driving into memory.

Or a warning.

Then—

"Whoa. Shit," Jesse said suddenly, braking hard.

The tires skidded slightly on the gravel and the truck shuddered to a stop. A tall pillar of dust rose up around them, hung in the air like smoke.

"Look," Jesse said, nodding forward.

Nate had already felt it—

a prickling cold along his arms,

his neck,

his spine—

before he even saw it.

Ahead of them, sprawled half across the dirt road, was a carcass.

At first, all Nate saw was **red**—

a wide smear, a grotesque tapestry of blood and pulp soaking into the damp earth. Then his eyes adjusted to the shapes above it: ribs like snapped branches, meat peeled back in strips, dark and glistening.

A moose. Or what used to be one.

Its belly had been split wide open, clean and deliberate, like a duffel bag unzipped with one swift motion. The ribs jutted out at wrong angles, slick and steaming slightly in the chill. Skin hung in loose, flayed curtains from the sides, swaying just a little in the breeze. And the eyes—

Gone.

Just two black hollows stared up at the sky, blank and accusing.

Around it, several crows lay dead in the grass. Their black feathers were soaked through with dark brown blood, making their bodies blend into the mud like shadows. A single bloodstained feather lifted and spun in the wind, dancing above the carnage like a slow-burning fuse.

Jesse was the first one out.

Then the man with the bracelets followed, boots crunching on the gravel.

"Jesus," Dale whispered from the back, trying to squeeze forward for a look.

Ryan whistled low, already jumping out ahead of Dale.

"Damn," he said, awe in his voice. "That's a hell of a sight. Wolves, maybe?"

Nate didn't move.

He just stared at the scene through the window, frozen. His breath felt thin, like the air had shifted without him noticing. His hands were cold. He couldn't tell if it was fear, revulsion, or something older and worse. His body refused to respond—like it knew something his mind hadn't caught up to yet.

Tyler tilted his head, squinting at the carcass.

"Brutal," he muttered. "But I've never seen anything quite like that. Maybe bears or... or—"

He trailed off, like even the rest of that thought didn't want to be spoken out loud.

Ryan turned, casting a look back through the open door at Nate, still sitting rigidly in his seat, hands clenched in his lap like he'd forgotten what to do with them.

Then he looked to Jesse.

"Your brother always this delicate, or is he just special today?"

For a moment, Jesse said nothing.

He just stared at Nate — eyes unreadable, mouth tightening ever so slightly.

Then his lip twitched.

Not quite a smirk. Not kindness either. Just that familiar, crooked pull — the same expression he wore when he didn't want to deal with something, when he let silence do the talking.

And for a heartbeat, something else passed between them — a flicker behind the eyes, the kind of thing you don't notice unless you know what to look for.

Not mockery.

But not defense, either.

Just *distance.*

And it landed like a shove.

Only a second—

But it cut deep.

Nate felt it—

like a small tear down the center of something he hadn't even realized was still intact.

He turned back toward the window.

And didn't say a word either.

Nate couldn't look away.

The blood didn't just stain the ground—it soaked it, as if the forest had opened its mouth and drunk deep. Every blade of grass shimmered red, trembling slightly in the wind, glistening like wet wires. A crow's wing, broken and limp, shifted with the breeze—bloodied feathers fluttering like a torn flag.

A fly crawled across what used to be an eye—no, not an eye. A socket. The eye had been ripped clean out, leaving only a dark, pulpy void.

And then—

One of the dead crows twitched. Just once.

It shouldn't have moved.

But it did.

Nate blinked hard, his pulse skipping.

A cold ripple slid down his spine as he shifted in his seat, suddenly aware of how tightly he was holding himself.

Maybe it was just his eyes playing tricks.

A nerve spasm. A trick of the wind.

But the unease settled deeper anyway, coiling low in his gut like something waking up.

Nate's eyes were drawn back to it, even as every instinct told him to look away.

He didn't want to, but he couldn't help it—

and again he felt the emptiness where its eyes had been,

those hollow sockets still fixed on him, as if the thing had never stopped watching.

He swallowed hard, throat tight.

Something bitter rose in his chest, sharp and acid, curling behind his tongue like smoke.

Then, with a dull metallic thud, the rifle case slid back down onto his leg.

He flinched, a sharp breath catching in his lungs.

"Wolves—or even a bear—don't rip out eyes," Jesse said, climbing back into the truck. "That's... that's something else."

He twisted in the seat to glance at Nate, forcing a casual tone into his voice, like he was replying to something Nate had said—though Nate hadn't said a word.

"Hey, uh... yeah, I mean—this is probably just some weird one-off thing, right? Like, a freak accident or whatever."

A beat.

"You good?"

Nate said nothing.

Just gave a quick nod and turned away from the grisly scene.

While the others clambered back into the truck, Nate stayed frozen, somewhere between breath and memory.

His vision tunneled.

The sound dropped out.

And then—

A flash.

The muzzle of a rifle.

A deafening crack.

Blood arcing through the air—hot, thick—splattering across his skin, his face, his hands.

He could still feel it.

Those tiny, burning droplets clinging to him, even now.

Memory or not, they hadn't cooled.

He flinched.

And then—

it was gone.

His phone buzzed in his jacket pocket. He jumped like he'd been shocked, sucked violently back into the present.

Voices filled the truck again.

Trees began to slide past outside the window.

He fumbled in his pockets, finally tugging the phone free.

On the screen: *Mia.*

Her smiling face lit up the glass, bright, soft, and terribly distant.

He couldn't help it—he smiled just a little.

Then swiped to answer.

"Hey. Just wanted to hear your voice," her voice came through, warm and clear. "You okay?"

"Yeah," he said, nodding more to himself than to her. "We're still driving. Everything's fine."

A pause.

Then, quieter:

"Just... I had a weird dream. Something bad. I've got this feeling, Nate. So if—"

The call cut off.

Just silence.

Dead air.

Nate stared at the screen. No signal.

Goosebumps raced up his arms.

He shook the phone uselessly, like maybe that would bring the connection back.

"Shit," he muttered, almost to himself.

The signal bar blinked out entirely.

He shut the phone off and shoved it back into his pocket.

The woods were deepening now.

The trees grew taller, older. More moss, thicker bramble. The road narrowed until it barely felt like one anymore. Fog crept from the underbrush in long, quiet tendrils, stretching across the dirt like something alive. The air turned wet. The light dimmed.

The headlights, once sharp, now glowed soft and useless, swallowed by mist.

And then—

The road simply ended.

No sign.

No marker.

Just earth.

The truck lurched to a stop. One final jolt.

The silence that followed was complete.

No birds.

No wind.

Just the soft, steady ticking of the cooling engine.

They got out.

Nate climbed out last, his boots crunching against the damp dirt. Cold air bit at his face, sharp and unwelcoming. Fog curled low over the ground, winding through the trees like it had a mind of its own. Nothing about this place looked serene or picturesque. It felt wrong. Too still. Too dark. As if the forest itself was holding its breath.

He zipped up his jacket, shivering—not just from the cold.

Around him, the others were already moving, loud and casual: unloading gear, cracking jokes. Coolers hit the ground with dull thuds. Rifles. Tents. Knives. Beer. Nate's eyes caught on the weapons and he took an unconscious step back, his stomach tightening. He looked up.

The trees towered above, unmoving. Not even a whisper of wind in their branches. They stood like silent watchers, frozen in time. In that eerie, motionless quiet, the others' chatter felt off. Loud. Wrong. Like sound that didn't belong here.

Near the back of the truck, Jesse glanced over.

«Listen,» he said quietly, rubbing the back of his neck. «Don't take it personal. I just didn't want them thinking you didn't belong. That's all. Don't be mad.»

Nate didn't look at him. «I do not belong.»

Jesse appeared beside him without warning, placing a hand on his shoulder. «You okay?»

Nate nodded, offering a crooked, dry smile. «Why does everyone keep asking me that?»

Jesse gave a soft huff of breath, almost a laugh. «I dunno. You just seem... I don't know. Off.»

He hesitated, studying Nate's face for a beat before glancing away.

«We all know why we're here,» Jesse said, his voice lower now. «And... I'm glad you came, Nate.»

But he didn't look him in the eye. Said it like he was afraid of the words, like they might mean more than he wanted.

Nate nodded slowly. «Yeah. Me too, I guess. It's just... what they said in the truck. Maybe they're right. Maybe I've been gone too long. Maybe I shouldn't have—»

«No,» Jesse cut in, his voice firm.

Then softer: «C'mon. You remember, right? Don't show weakness. Not out here.»

He let that hang for a second, then added, more quietly:

«They'll eat you alive if you do. We're surrounded by real predators now.»

That brought Nate's gaze to him sharply.

He frowned. «And that... impresses you? Is that what I'm hearing?»

Jesse gave a short, deflective laugh and patted his shoulder.

«Drop it. You're here. We're together. And you've got just as much reason to be as any of us. Dad would've wanted that.»

He paused.

«You know what he'd say, right now?»

Nate huffed, the ghost of a nod. «Being afraid's fine. Just don't let them see it.»

He turned his head, looking out into the deep woods stretching before them.

«You're not a hunter till you know what it feels like to be prey.»

And as he said it, he could almost hear his father's voice echo the words, not from memory—closer. Like he was right there beside him.

Jesse nodded. «Exactly. And more than that... hunting's an honest game, son. You win, or you die. That's the deal.»

He looked at Nate again.

«He'd be proud of you, you know. Just for standing here.»

Nate blinked, caught off guard. Something in the way Jesse said it landed hard. The words didn't just settle in his chest—they lodged there.

For a while, Nate stood still, watching them as they moved around the truck, voices rising and falling in short bursts of laughter and orders. Jesse walked ahead, calling something over his shoulder, already vanishing between the trunks.

Nate followed.

He stumbled a little, boots catching in the uneven ground, his legs stiff like they'd forgotten how to walk. The trees seemed to lean closer, their branches crowding together like whispers overhead. Dark leaves. Dark bark. The same forest in every direction. No path. No signs. Just woods.

The forest took him in.

And did not say a word.

Behind him, the road was gone. Not ended—vanished. Swallowed by roots and mist and shadow, as if it had never existed at all.

There was no going back. Not really.

Chapter 2:
The One Who Hunts Hunters

Twilight fell like a slow exhale—the kind that empties everything out. The sky over the Appalachians bled into a deep, bruised purple as shadows rose from the forest floor like something summoned. One moment, a faint trace of gold still shimmered above the treetops. The next—it was gone. Like a switch had been flipped. The sun didn't set; it disappeared. No ceremony. No grace. Just an abrupt plunge into black.

And there was nothing beautiful about this night.

Darkness poured into the woods, thick and unapologetic, staining every tree, every stone, every breath. The forest transformed in seconds. What had been green and familiar hours before now stood black and unknowable, a wall of bark and needles and silence. The trees closed in—tighter, heavier—as if something ancient and massive had rolled over the mountains and spread its limbs across the land.

There was something in them now. Something new. Something wrong.

The forest was breathing. Not just with wind or the rustling of squirrels, but with something deeper. It exhaled dread. Inhaled memory. It was watching.

They'd made camp beside a narrow creek that murmured and trickled over cold, mossy rocks, its voice too soft to matter anymore. The tents were uneven, flaps sagging open, sleeping bags half-unrolled. Gear lay scattered like a half-forgotten ritual. A few empty beer cans already glittered in the firelight.

The fire hissed and popped, fighting for space in the dark. Its flames flared up in brief defiance, casting shadows that danced like they were afraid to get too far from the warmth. Sparks spiraled upward—and vanished. Swallowed whole by the velvet dark above.

Night had settled like a predator.

And into that dark bled laughter. Loud. Unchecked. Careless.

Voices echoed—too bright, too sharp. Jokes cut through the thick air like knives. Some were funny, some cruel. All of it too much, too alive against the weight of the woods. Like they were trying to drown out something deeper with their noise.

But the silence between laughs? That was where the forest waited.

A soft mist had begun to spill in from the brush, creeping along the ground in faint blue ribbons. It wasn't heavy. It didn't blind. It simply was. Quiet and inevitable, like it belonged here far more than they did.

Someone cracked open another beer.

Tyler was already sitting by the fire, of course. He'd claimed his place early, a half-empty flask resting beside his boot, bracelets clinking quietly as he shifted. He leaned back on one elbow, legs stretched into the dirt, the firelight painting gold into the stubble on his jaw.

But it was his eyes that gave him away. They never stopped moving. They tracked everything—every flicker, every rustle, every breath from someone's lips. He looked like a man who expected something to leap from the trees at any moment. Or worse, like someone wanted it to.

"There's no such thing as a bloodless forest," Tyler said suddenly, his voice low and sharp, like the crack of a dry twig. "Y'all know that, right?"

The others didn't answer. Not right away. A bottle clinked. Laughter somewhere behind Nate faded out.

Tyler swept his gaze slowly around the circle.

"We all saw it," he said, eyes glinting in the fire. "That moose. Or whatever the hell it was. Ripped wide open. Eyes gone. Like something took them."

He paused. Let the silence bite.

"Some folks would say that's messed up. Scary, even."

His voice dropped an octave. Thick with mockery.

"Maybe even wet their pants a little."

He turned his eyes to Nate.

The glance wasn't long. Didn't need to be. Just enough for everyone to catch it.

"Out here, that's the price. You step into the woods—real woods, not your backyard shit—you'd better be ready for blood. That's the rule. That's always been the rule."

The fire cracked.

He leaned forward, elbows on his knees.

"See, the forest doesn't care if you're scared. Doesn't care if you didn't mean it. If you cry. If you run."

His voice softened, almost like a bedtime story.

"You bleed, or you take blood. That's the deal. That's always been the deal."

He let that sit for a second.

Then he smiled. Not wide. Not warm. Just a flick of teeth in the firelight.

"And if you don't like it," he whispered, "the forest eats you."

He leaned back, a smug gleam in his eye, and raised the flask to his lips like he'd just delivered a prophecy.

"Oh hell yeah," Ryan jumped in, his eyes flashing with something too eager— like the very word blood lit up a part of him that didn't get to speak too often. He was crouched low near the fire, knees bent like a hunter ready to spring. He'd been drinking steadily for hours, but somehow it didn't show. Or maybe it just didn't matter. His edges stayed sharp. Dangerous.

He tipped his bottle back again, taking a few long gulps. Some of it spilled past the corner of his mouth, trickling down his chin and splashing onto the dirt between his boots.

"I like that mindset. Hell, I respect it," he said, nodding to himself like he'd just solved a moral equation. His voice sliced through the night like a sawblade—too loud, too certain. "If you're afraid of blood, you've got no damn business being in places like this."

He let out a sound that wasn't quite a laugh—more like a grunt, a snort. Self-satisfied.

Dale gave a little grunt of his own and blinked at Ryan like he'd just realized he was there. "Yeah... yeah, man. I heard that too, y'know? Guy with the gun's the one who owns the woods." He broke into a laugh that shook his whole body, his cheeks wobbling like jello in a truck bed.

Jesse gave a lopsided smile, squinting into the flames. "Nah. One gun's not enough out here."

"Then the king of the woods is the guy with more bullets!" Dale barked, laughing even harder at his own joke, slapping his knee with one hand and nearly toppling over.

Nate sat a little ways off, beer in hand. Not far. But not close either. Watching.

The beer was lukewarm now, bitter. The can slick in his fingers, sweating like his palms. He took a sip—half reflex, half attempt to feel something normal. The bitter cold of it shocked his mouth, snapped him slightly back into himself.

But the tightness didn't leave. Not inside. Not around him.

It was like being wrapped in invisible twine, a hundred threads pulling inward. Something pressing down. Quietly. Constantly.

The woods around them loomed, closer than they had any right to be—like they'd leaned in while no one was watching. The air was thick with woodsmoke, wet moss, and something else—something sour, faint, like old meat, like the forest had a wound somewhere out there, and it was festering.

Then—a *rustle*.

Soft, but not soft enough. Nate flinched. Looked toward the trees. No one else reacted. Just more laughter. More jokes. Another beer cracking open. Another voice shouting something that sounded like bravado.

But that sound… That had been real.

He tried to let it go. Really, he tried.

But it was like sitting on a tightrope strung above something bottomless. The laughter around him wasn't comforting. It was sharp. Brittle. Like glass clinking before it shatters. And every creak in the branches beyond the fire's light felt like a breath held too long. Like something waiting to exhale.

Tyler spoke again.

"No," he said, voice softer now, like a warning not meant for all ears. The fire caught the glint of his bracelets as he shifted. "I'm not talking about blood, not really."

His tone was different. Slower. Measured.

He swept that blind eye of his around the circle, and it was almost worse than if he could see. Like something unseen was staring through him and out the other side.

"It's about the moment," he said. "You step into a place like this, and it wraps around you. Like a noose." He lifted one hand slowly, curling his fingers into a fist. "Every breath, every damn twig snap—it tightens."

"You either make it out… or you don't."

He took a swig from his bottle, spit into the dark, and grinned like a man remembering something delicious.

"You could have a million bullets. But one wrong step, and you're just another blind moose with its eyes ripped out."

He chuckled to himself and gave a short snort, satisfied. "You just have to feel it."

Dale blinked. "Feel what?"

"Oh Jesus," Ryan snapped. "You really are a moron, Dale."

He turned his head suddenly, barking across the fire, "Hey, Nate!"

Nate looked up slowly.

Ryan was grinning wide. Teeth catching the firelight. "You get what we're saying here?"

Nate raised his brows—not in surprise, but to keep something else from showing on his face. Something colder.

He forced a smile.

"Yeah," he said, voice quiet but steady. "Seems pretty clear."

He took another sip of his beer and glanced at the fire.

"I'm just surrounded by blood-happy psychos. Nothing I haven't seen before."

Ryan smiled wide—but it wasn't friendly. It wasn't even smug. It was cruel, curled at the corners like something meant to cut.

"Oh, yeah," he said, almost with delight. "I figured it'd be something like that. And I was right." He flicked a glance at Jesse, then back to Nate. "Your brother's soft, man. Like a goddamn schoolgirl."

He raised the bottle to his lips, took a long pull, then let it fall against his knee with a hollow thunk.

"I'm not one for sugarcoating," Ryan said, his voice rough and sharp. "So here it is—Nate, you should've kept your soft ass at home, where it's safe and quiet."

He let the words hang in the air, like a challenge he wanted someone to take up.

Then he let out a sound—half growl, half laugh. Nate couldn't quite tell which. Didn't care to ask.

He gave a thin, unreadable smile in response. No words. Just silence, thick and deliberate.

Ryan sat sprawled out, one leg stretched toward the fire, the other crooked lazily like he owned the ground beneath him. His shoulders filled the space, casting long, jagged shadows in the firelight. His gaze moved slowly across the group—measured, heavy—like a judge weighing each man's worth before handing down the verdict.

"Hunters," he said, with weight behind the word. "That's who runs these woods. That's who decides what gets to live and what doesn't. We come in, and we take what we want. Every damn time."

There was a pride in his tone, but something else too—something rough and jagged beneath it. Something dangerous.

Nate swallowed. The voice grated through him, like a bad memory. And behind that voice came the clumsy giggle of Dale, the twisted grin of Tyler—bracelets chiming like wind chimes in a storm. And just for a breath, Nate's eyes met Jesse's across the fire.

He was trying—really trying—to find something in this moment worth holding onto. Something warm in the fire, something steady in the beer, something grounding in the pine smoke. Anything that would make this feel like a good idea. Like he belonged here.

But the woods pressed in too tight. The laughter was too brittle. The fire was too small.

Then Jesse moved, almost instinctively, like he felt it too. He shuffled closer and sat beside Nate with a slow grunt, holding his beer in both hands. He nudged Nate's boot gently with his own.

"Relax, city boy," he said.

Nate smirked, barely.

But Jesse's eyes stayed serious. Then he raised his beer a little higher, voice cutting through the murmur of fire and laughter.

"I just wanna remind everyone why we're out here."

The group quieted. Eyes turned.

Ryan's gaze slid sideways toward Nate again. Nate felt it—sharp as a blade—but didn't look back.

Jesse nodded once. "Our old man... he loved this. The cold. The woods. The stories. The hunt." His voice softened just slightly. "I think we all miss him. And I know he'd appreciate us being here tonight."

He lifted his can higher.

"To Robert Briggs. The real hunter."

There was a small pause—then voices joined in:

"To Briggs!"

Nate raised his can. Hesitated. Then drank.

The beer tasted different now. Like ash. As if something had changed it in the last five minutes.

"He wasn't just a hunter," Nate said, his voice quieter. Not to the crowd, but more to the fire. "He taught us things. Me, especially. How to keep your hands steady. How to breathe through fear. How not to run."

Ryan snorted. "Taught you not to run? Didn't look like it stuck."

There were a few laughs. Not Jesse's. Nate didn't even blink.

"I still remember what he said once," Nate continued. "'Courage isn't being unafraid. It's knowing the thing's gonna kill you… and standing there anyway.'"

Tyler nodded, his face for once free of mockery.

"He said that to me too. Right before we tracked that cougar up near Devil's Ridge," he murmured. "Hunting with him... man, it was something else. He never missed. Not once. Can you even imagine that?"

Ryan barked a sharp laugh, leaning back as if the whole conversation had been one long setup for his punchline.

"Oh, come on," he said, eyes gleaming in the firelight. "Bob Briggs wasn't some backwoods philosopher. He was a drunk with a rifle and a mean streak. Don't go dressing him up like he was Yoda."

The fire cracked, sending a brief burst of sparks skyward. Jesse turned his head slowly, his expression shifting—eyes narrowing, shoulders going still.

"Careful, Ry."

Ryan smirked, not backing down for a second.

"What? I'm just saying—he wasn't some wise old sage. He liked the hunt. He liked killing things. Let's not sugarcoat the man."

Jesse's mouth opened, just slightly—like he was on the verge of saying something. Maybe a defense. Maybe an agreement. But the moment was crushed under the weight of Dale's voice, slurred and sudden.

"Gentlemen," Dale announced, holding up one finger like he was about to bless the firepit, "enough of the dead-dad drama. Let's talk about something fun for once."

He laughed—alone at first, then others joined in. The tension cracked like a dry branch underfoot. The heat in the air broke. The moment scattered.

But Nate...

Nate felt it slip *through his fingers.*

Something sharp and voiceless inside him screamed, like a violin string pulled too tight. Something recoiled. But something else stirred. Shifted. Moved sideways like a shadow changing shape in torchlight. He didn't understand it yet, not fully—but it felt like someone had scraped their fingernails across the most vulnerable part of him.

And it had rung like a bell.

One more word, one more second, and it might've rung back.

But he held it.

Then—

A **rustle.**

Soft. Wet. Wrong.

Not wind. Not squirrel.

From the trees.

All at once, the group froze. Jesse's head snapped toward the sound. Tyler sat up straighter, bracelets softly clinking. Ryan's hand reached instinctively for the flashlight clipped to his belt—but paused just long enough to brush the stock of his rifle.

One breath.

Two.

The fire crackled. A log shifted.

Then Dale laughed again, snorting as he wiped at his nose with the back of his sleeve.

"Relax. Probably just a raccoon with performance anxiety."

The moment dissolved, but only on the surface. The others chuckled, shoulders loosening, conversation rising again in fits and waves. But the fire burned just a little lower.

Nate didn't laugh.

He kept watching the trees.

The darkness beyond the firelight wasn't empty. It felt crowded. Thick. A presence more than a space. The forest no longer seemed still—it seemed watchful. The trees stood like sentinels, unmoving, but somehow full of sound. Deep, distant sounds. Wet footfalls. The creak of heavy wood. Things too heavy to be birds. Too real to be dreams.

Still… *maybe it was all in his head. Maybe it really was just a raccoon. Or the beer.*

He'd never liked places like this. Not even as a kid. Never liked the silence that wasn't really silent. Never liked the smell of blood in the air after a kill. Even watching someone clean a fish made his stomach twist.

Nate shivered again. The beer in his hand was gone. Warm, metallic, and bitter.

He tipped the can, felt the emptiness.

With a slow breath, he reached for another. The hiss of the tab breaking the seal was loud in the quiet.

He didn't look away from the treeline.

Not yet.

Tyler leaned forward, elbows resting on his knees. The firelight caught in his eyes, turning them glassy and strange—like something was moving behind them that didn't quite belong.

"You ever hear what happened to Jim Davis?" he asked, voice low and a little too casual. Like a question asked from behind a closed door.

Ryan groaned. "Oh Jesus. Here we go again."

But Jesse didn't look away. "No, let him talk," he said. "Jim went missing last fall. Right near these woods."

Tyler nodded, slow and deliberate. "Went out hunting," he said. "Never came back. Dogs picked up his scent for about a mile... then it just stopped. No blood, no bootprints, no broken brush. Just... gone. Like he got erased."

Dale chuckled. "Abducted by sexy aliens."

Tyler didn't even blink. "I heard something else," he went on. "From someone who used to hunt with him. Said Jim was tracking something that day. A boar. Not just any pig—huge. Bigger than a bear. Blacker than asphalt. The kind of black that doesn't reflect light. Said the ground shook when it moved."

Ryan snorted again, tipping his head back. "Come on, man."

But Tyler's voice dropped, smoothing into something darker. "They found his knife later. Lodged in a tree trunk. Like he'd thrown it—hard. Blade was bent nearly in half. No blood. No body. Just... tracks."

Nate's mouth opened before he could stop it. "What kind of tracks?"

Tyler turned his head toward him. The firelight danced in his good eye.

"Too big," he said. "Too clean. Too... symmetrical. Like something walking that had studied footsteps, not made them."

The fire popped. And for a second, nobody spoke.

Then—

Crack.

A branch snapped out in the trees.

This time, it didn't sound like a raccoon. Or wind. Or imagination.

It sounded like something heavy. Something that waited until the silence hit its deepest point—and then answered.

Every head turned.

Jesse straightened slowly, beer halfway to his mouth. Tyler didn't move. Ryan shifted, muttering something under his breath and brushing his hand against the rifle beside him.

"Probably a deer," he said too quickly. Then added, with a crooked grin, "Though if it's that symmetrical, I'd love to shoot the bastard. Hang it over the fireplace just for the weird factor."

He snorted—a harsh, guttural sound that didn't match the tension in his jaw.

Then—

A breath.

Low. Wet. Close.

Like something just behind the treeline had leaned forward and exhaled. Not an animal sound, not quite. There was intention in it. Weight.

Nate felt it first. Even before the others stiffened.

He stared into the dark, eyes wide, ears straining. But there was nothing to see—just a wall of black trees and the hiss of wind threading through dead branches.

Still, the sound clung to him. Like breath on the back of his neck.

No one moved. Not for a full ten seconds.

Then—

Nothing.

The woods fell quiet again, too quiet. Like something had retreated—but not far.

Tyler broke the silence with a laugh. Short. Dry.

"Forest games," he said, lifting the bottle again. "This place has a sense of humor."

He drank deep, wiped his mouth on his sleeve, then leaned closer to the flames. His voice came out softer now. More deliberate. The kind of tone used by someone about to tell a secret.

"Alright," he said. "You want a real story? Since we're all so interested in who really owns this forest..."

He paused, letting the fire crackle between them.

"I can tell you."

He shifted again, the light flaring across the curve of his bracelets as they chimed against each other. One eye—the good one—gleamed like polished stone. The other remained blind, milky and still.

"There's a legend around here," he said. "Old as the dirt. My granddad told it to me. His granddad told it to him. And this forest? It remembers."

His voice thinned to a whisper, but it didn't lose strength. If anything, it grew heavier, as though the trees themselves were leaning in to listen.

"This forest," he said again. "*This* one."

For a brief second, Nate caught Jesse's gaze through the fire.

Jesse wasn't smiling anymore. He was watching Tyler—hard. Focused. Like a man leaning forward toward the edge of something.

Nate looked back at Tyler. He didn't know why.

Maybe it was curiosity. Maybe it was dread. But something in him leaned forward, too. Not physically. Not consciously. But *something* in his chest—something old and tight and coiled—tugged toward the firelight.

Tyler didn't raise his voice, but something about the way he spoke cut through the crackling fire and the half-drunken laughter. His tone dipped into something colder—older. His blind eye glinted for a second in the flicker of the flames, catching the light like a dead star.

"They say there's something out here," he began. "Not a bear. Not a wolf. Not even a man. They call it the Blood Tusker. The Boar That Hunts Back. The One Who Hunts Hunters. A spirit. A punishment. A reckoning in flesh."

Ryan gave a dry laugh and lifted the last of his bottle. He drank it down in one long pull, then hurled the empty into the brush with a careless grunt. Almost before it landed, he was reaching for the next.

Dale chuckled, halfhearted. "Sounds like a metal band."

Tyler didn't blink.

"A long time ago," he continued, "back when these hills didn't have names and cabins were just planks and prayers, there was a rule: take what you need. No more. Hunt to eat, not to conquer. Kill with thanks—not laughter."

The fire popped. Sparks spiraled into the dark like fleeting spirits.

"Those who broke that rule... the forest took notice. And when it did, it sent something. Something massive. Bristled black as ash. Silent as snowfall. Eyes like smoldering coals. Tusks like bone blades—not two, but many. Like a crown. It didn't growl. Didn't snarl. It just appeared. And tore men apart like wet paper."

Ryan scoffed, the firelight dancing in his pupils with a kind of wild thrill. "Jesus. Really?" he barked. "So where do I sign up to meet this thing?"

Dale let out a hiccup of laughter, but it rang flat. Forced.

Tyler pressed on, unshaken.

"It didn't show itself often. Only when the balance tipped. When hunters forgot the rules. When blood became a game. When laughter followed the kill. That's when it came. And no one who saw it... ever lived long enough to say what it looked like."

He glanced up, his gaze sweeping them all.

"Except one. Elijah Crane. Old man. Lived up near Copper Ridge. Claimed he saw it once. Said it looked him right in the eye... and walked away."

"Why?" Jesse asked, his voice barely above a whisper.

"Crane said it smelled sorrow on him. Said it only kills the proud. The cruel. The ones who think the woods belong to them."

This time, no one laughed.

A silence settled over the group—not just quiet, but weighted. Like the forest had paused to listen.

The fire crackled, small and uncertain, like it too was waiting.

No one spoke. Even the wind seemed to hold its breath.

Somewhere deep in the trees, something shifted—too far to see, too close to forget.

For one long moment, the forest listened.

Tyler's voice softened, almost reverent now. "So when we talk about how blood and forest are bound together... just remember. We may hunt. But nature decides who leaves. And who doesn't."

Even Ryan didn't speak right away.

Eventually, he snorted, brushing off the quiet with a cough. He fumbled for a cigarette, found one, and lit it with a sharp flick of his lighter. The flame briefly lit the hard line of his jaw.

Then, suddenly, he spat: "Great story. Real spooky. But if this thing's real? Bring it on. You show me a beast, I'll drop it in one shot." He leaned back and tapped his temple with the cigarette. "Especially if it's got hooves the size of buckets. That'd look great mounted over my fireplace. Or hell, maybe the kitchen. Real conversation piece."

He reached for his rifle, lifted it like a toast.

"You shoot it," Tyler said quietly, "and maybe it lets you think you've won. Until it tears you open in your sleep."

Then, just as quickly, he smirked. "Hell of a tale, huh? You should've seen your faces, boys."

But his laugh was cut short.

A breeze passed through the camp. Not strong. Just enough to make the flames waver and the trees whisper. It moved like something with purpose. Like something was circling.

Leaves rustled. Branches creaked.

Nobody moved.

Dale let out a sharp breath, part snort, part nervous chuckle. "Alright, that's enough bedtime stories for me. Anybody got marshmallows?"

Jesse stood and stretched, bones cracking in the quiet. "I'm turning in," he muttered.

The camp began to dissolve—slow, drunken shuffling, the rustle of tent zippers, the thud of boots against packed earth. Shapes moved like ghosts around the dimming firelight, everyone suddenly too eager to find the safety of nylon and zippers. Even the laughter had dimmed, as if the trees had taken it in and held it tight.

Nate stood too, wordless, and lit a cigarette with a trembling hand. The flame flared, brief and weak, then vanished into smoke. He drew in deep, held it, then exhaled into the dark—toward the trees. Toward something.

Something shifted out there. Not loud. Just enough to catch his ear.

He froze, squinting. Nothing but black. The trees stood motionless, and yet... it felt like something behind them had moved in response. Like the forest had taken a breath of its own.

He told himself it was nerves. Unfamiliar ground. Too many drinks. The camp. The stories. But there was something about this place—something *off.* As if the earth here remembered footsteps that hadn't returned.

His father had walked these woods.

That thought clung to him as he crushed out the cigarette and ducked into the tent.

The fire was just a whisper now. Outside, the trees leaned closer. Pressed in. The dark made them seem infinite—like columns of a cathedral built to hold silence instead of prayer.

He lay there, eyes wide, staring up at the roof of the tent. But he wasn't seeing nylon. He was seeing his father.

The old man's voice drifted back through years like fog over water.

"You're not a hunter till you know what it feels like to be prey," he'd once said. His tone steady. Quiet. Spoken in the stillness of dawn, somewhere deep in the woods. "You gotta know how it feels. How the breath catches. How every sound is a gunshot in your mind."

Nate smiled, just a little. A bitter, reluctant thing.

Damn, he thought. *He was a real hunter.*

And tonight, those words returned. Not just memory—presence. Like they'd been waiting.

Far off, a branch cracked. Sharp. Sudden.

Nate's body went still. Breath caught in his throat. He raised his head, slowly.

Another sound—a breath. Not his own. Wet. Close. Impossible.

He turned his head toward it. Nothing.

Still... every hair on his body rose.

He crept to the flap of the tent and peeked out. The night was deep. Total. The trees had become walls. Still, unmoving, but filled with a silence that felt full.

Nothing stirred.

But he could feel it.

Eyes.

Watching.

Waiting.

Chapter 3:

Deeper into the Dark

The forest was silent in the way only ancient things can be.

Cold breath lingered over the morning earth, and dew clung to every blade of grass like an unspoken warning. The fire had long since died, leaving behind only the faintest threads of smoke curling through the air like fading spirits. Above, the trees held the sky hostage—just jagged silhouettes against a bruised smear of mist and cloud. It was morning, technically. But no light reached the forest floor without a fight.

Nate was the first to rise.

Not because he wanted to, or because he felt particularly disciplined. But because sleep had fractured under the weight of memory. What dreams came were heavy and jagged, like falling through ice into something far older and darker than sleep should allow. He'd jolted awake at every shift in the trees, every snap of twig and breath of wind that might have been something else entirely. And always, always, he emerged from the blackness of sleep with the sense that something had been watching him—too close, too still.

He crawled out of the tent, his breath fogging in the cold. The air had bite this morning—crisp, metallic, sharp like the forest was baring its teeth.

His boots, still too new, looked wrong against the mud and moss. Laces tied tight, spotless just yesterday, they were now stained at the edges with damp earth. A small thing. But enough to remind him he didn't belong here—not like the others. Not like Jesse or Ryan. The forest rejected him in small ways, through the chill in his spine and the unease in his lungs.

He splashed his face with icy water and stood for a while, arms crossed, cigarette trembling slightly between his fingers. When he exhaled, the smoke curled upward and forward, pulled into the hush of the woods like an offering. It twisted in strange spirals, disrupted only by a breeze too cold for summer.

The trees didn't move. Didn't sway. They just stood. Watching.

He stared into them, lips tight, jaw working. As if waiting for them to speak. To reveal something. But they said nothing. Just that same mute pressure, as though the forest knew him—knew what he'd done. And didn't quite forgive.

He took another drag. The smoke tasted bitter this morning. Not like tobacco, but like memory.

Then he saw it.

Something in the dirt.

He stepped forward, heart suddenly ticking louder. One boot. Then the next. And the forest—impossibly—seemed to hold its breath with him. The morning mist clung to the ground like cobwebs, and the wet hush of dawn made every motion feel sacrilegious. Nate squinted downward.

Tracks.

Deep impressions in the soft earth, half-filled with water and still rimmed with the ragged shine of crushed leaves. He frowned and crouched slightly. They were hoofed, sure—but not like deer. Not even moose. Too broad. Too deep. The soil around them was torn open in places, like the ground had tried to resist being stepped on. One print had a strange splay to it, as if the hoof had twisted mid-stride, wrenching sideways under some impossible weight. Another—deeper still—looked layered, like a second step had landed right inside the first, pushing it down with purpose.

No animal should've been that heavy. Not even a bull moose in rut.

The impressions didn't just rest on the surface—they sank into it. As though whatever left them wasn't walking so much as pressing itself into the world.

Nate's skin prickled. He didn't know why exactly. Just that something was wrong. Fundamentally. His breath puffed in the chill air, curling like smoke above the prints.

"Morning," Jesse muttered behind him, still rubbing the sleep from his eyes.

"How'd you sleep?" Nate asked without looking up.

"Like shit."

"I barely slept at all," Nate said quietly, and took a slow drag from his cigarette. The smoke curled between them, gray and steady. His eyes never left the ground. "Come look at this."

Jesse blinked, then stepped forward, following Nate's line of sight. His frown deepened. He crouched low and stared for a long moment.

"...The hell?" he muttered. "What is that?"

"I heard something last night," Nate said. "Branches. Movement. Like... weight. Didn't think much of it. But now..."

Behind them, the camp began to stir. Sleeping bags crinkled. Zippers rasped like small, metallic sighs. Someone cursed the cold, dragging boots through damp needles. The groggy rustle of bodies roused from half-sleep filled the clearing like the hush before a storm. One by one, they emerged—blinking, yawning, scratching at stubble and shaking off dreams like ash—then wandered closer, drawn not by curiosity but something quieter. Heavier.

Soon they were all circling Jesse, the tracks at his feet pulling them inward like iron filings to a buried magnet.

They gathered close, heads bent over the prints, like a pack of dogs scenting not prey, but something older.

"What the...?" Ryan's voice cut through the stillness. His eyes lit up the moment they landed on the tracks. He sniffed the air reflexively, boots crunching as he stepped forward like a bloodhound pulling a scent from the dirt.

He crouched low, nostrils flaring.

"Hoo boy," he said with a low whistle. "Something big's been through here." He glanced around, suddenly alert. "And I mean big."

Jesse leaned in again, tracing the rim of the largest track with his fingertip. "Could be a moose," he offered, but even he didn't sound like he believed it. "I mean... a real old one. Big bastard."

Dale grunted, arms crossed. "Moose with feet like that?" He squinted, then gave one of his trademark dumb-laugh grins. "What's next, raccoons with sneakers?"

He laughed at his own joke—loud, wheezy, and alone. Nobody joined in.

Then Tyler stepped closer.

Silent.

He crouched slowly, gaze locked on the earth. Something shifted in his face— not surprise, not confusion, but a tightening. Nate caught it: the faintest twitch at the corner of his mouth, the way his good eye narrowed just slightly.

Tyler reached out and dragged his fingers lightly over the edge of the track. Then he just sat there. Still. Not blinking. Not speaking.

The silence stretched.

He lit a cigarette without taking his eyes off the ground.

A long drag. Exhale. Still staring.

Then, quietly—like the words had been steeped in the soil and smoked dry— he muttered, "This ain't no moose."

Everyone turned.

Nate's voice came out low, rough. "Then what is it?"

Jesse crouched low, one hand braced against his knee, the other hovering above the track like it might bite. His brow furrowed beneath the shadow of his cap.

"These hooves... they're too wide," he murmured. "Only thing in these woods with feet like that is a moose. And not just any moose. A damn giant."

Ryan snorted, spitting into the dirt without looking. "I don't care if it's a goddamn dinosaur," he said, already slinging his pack over one shoulder. "Let's follow it."

They packed in a hurry. Not frantic—but there was a knot in it. A tension that lived in their hands, made zippers snag and buckles rattle too loud. The kind of urgency that didn't want to call itself fear. Just... motion. Forward. Always forward.

Nate stood slightly apart, his pack slung loose, watching their faces.

Tyler was quiet, slower than the rest. His one good eye was distant, as if it was watching something behind the trees instead of in front of them. Something old. Something he'd seen before.

But Ryan—

Ryan was nearly *vibrating.*

He grabbed his rifle like it was part of him, his fingers tight around the grip—not with caution, but with pleasure. His gear hit the earth and rebounded. He moved like a man wound too tight, filled to the brim with something hot and dangerous. His eyes sparkled—not with adrenaline, but with anticipation. Hunger. The kind that made Nate's stomach clench.

There was something feral about him in that moment.

Predator, not man.

Nate couldn't look away.

The rest of them—Dale's muttering, Jesse's steady hands, Tyler's silence—they all blurred into the background. Like the forest had pulled them back a step. All sound distant. All movement muffled.

Then, for just a moment, Tyler looked up and caught Nate's eye.

Something in that glance was... hollow. Dimmed. As if whatever light had once lived behind it had grown weary. Faded into some deep and private place.

He said nothing.

Didn't need to.

They moved quickly and quiet, boots crunching damp leaves, shouldering into the thickening woods. The tracks led them forward like a trail of old scars. And the forest deepened around them.

Trees rose higher. **Pressed inward.**

The trunks stood close as cathedral columns, their bark slick with nightdew, blackened and cold. Above, the sky had vanished—replaced by interlocking limbs that filtered the sun into narrow, useless threads. Light that touched nothing. Lit nothing.

It was morning, but it felt like dusk.

Nate walked in the rear.

Not out of caution. Out of weight.

His legs moved, but each step felt harder than the last. Like the ground wanted to hold him. Like it remembered him.

His boots sank slightly in the loam. Wet, soft. The scent of rot grew stronger here—moldering leaves, damp moss, the faint, ghostly trace of something metallic. Old blood, maybe. Or worse.

He swallowed. His throat was dry.

It felt like they were descending.

Not in elevation—but in essence. As if the forest were a funnel, drawing them inward, downward. Into something darker. Something waiting.

A pit that wasn't dug, but grown.

He looked around.

Trees. Just trees.

But they were wrong now. Taller. Grimmer. Cloaked in fog and green-black moss that curled like smoke up their sides. The undergrowth had thickened, vines snaking underfoot, slick and whispering.

There was no path.

Only *direction.*

And with every step, Nate felt it tightening—his chest, his breath, his thoughts. The unease wasn't fear, not yet.

It was the space fear lives in before it gets a name.

Something was watching.

Not from the branches.

Not from the shadows.

But from the silence itself.

And the silence was walking with them.

Branches cracked beneath their boots, dew brushing their legs, and somewhere a crow cried into the dull, gray morning.

Jesse caught up beside him, his jacket damp at the shoulders from the clinging mist.

"Hey," Jesse said, voice low as he came up beside him. "You figured out where we're headed yet?"

Nate didn't look over. Just gave a small nod. "The place."

Jesse smirked a little. "Yeah. The place. You remember Dad's stories, right? Called it a hunter's paradise. Boars, moose, red foxes... like something out of a damn fairy tale."

Nate nodded again, slower this time. His brow furrowed. "If it's a fairy tale, it's the kind where everyone gets lost in the woods. Honestly? I've got a bad feeling. Like... we might not be coming back out."

He tried to pass it off with a shrug, but it landed too heavy, sat between them like a weight.

Jesse's smile faded. He nodded, quiet for a second. "That's kind of the point, isn't it? We're going where he went. Feels like... the right way to honor him."

Nate stopped. "What are you saying?"

Jesse hesitated, then turned to face him, keeping his voice low. "Just thinking out loud. Feels like we're closing the loop, you know? I was thinking... maybe you carry a rifle. Just this once. For Dad. For the anniversary."

"No." Nate said it quick, clipped. His shoulders stiffened.

Jesse exhaled. "He'd want you to."

"Jess, stop." Nate shook his head. "You wanna honor him? Great. Fire all the shots you want. But don't drag me into it."

His voice dropped, firm now. "I'm not him. And I'm not you. He lived for this shit. I never did. I don't want to."

Jesse took a step closer, dropping his voice to a whisper. "Come on, man. It's been twenty years. You really gonna let that one thing define everything? It was an accident. A messed up, horrible accident, but it wasn't your fault. You've got to let that go."

Nate stared at him, eyes unreadable. "Jess... you don't get to decide when or how I let go. You wanted me here. I came. That's all I've got to give."

Jesse grimaced, opened his mouth to speak—but the words never came.

Somewhere ahead, a sound tore through the stillness. It wasn't just noise—it was violence made audible. A wet, guttural squeal rose through the trees, beginning as a hiss, then cracking open into something sharp and ragged. Underneath it came the crash of underbrush, branches snapping, something heavy thrashing through the undergrowth. The forest, moments ago muted and watchful, erupted into motion.

Nate turned sharply toward the sound, adrenaline flooding his veins. Ryan was already moving—no hesitation, no question. He charged forward like a man who'd been waiting his whole life for this exact moment. For a second, Nate didn't even recognize the speed in his limbs. He vanished between the trees in a blur of motion.

The others followed, boots pounding wet soil. Jesse. Dale. Even Tyler, silent and focused, his jaw clenched as he sprinted. Nate went last, trailing behind as the noise grew louder, sharper—less like an animal call and more like something screaming to survive.

The trees opened into a shallow clearing, and Nate pushed past the last curtain of branches just in time to see it.

The boar.

It was huge. Thick-bodied and ragged, its hide bristled and soaked in blood.

One flank was torn wide open, red spilling down its side in sluggish rivers. It pressed itself against the base of a tree, frothing, gasping, its dark eyes rolling white with panic. Foam and blood flecked its snout as it huffed in terror. It didn't charge. It didn't run. It just trembled, snarled, and held its ground like a cornered ghost.

Nate froze.

He took a step forward. Not out of courage—just a strange compulsion to understand what he was looking at. The wound wasn't from a bullet. It looked torn. Ripped. Like something had gotten to it first.

Ryan raised his rifle.

"Wait—" Nate's voice broke out, hand lifting to stop him.

Too late.

The gunshot cracked like thunder. A spray of blood burst outward, hot and immediate. Nate jerked as if struck himself. Tiny flecks hit his face and his arm—warm and wet—and for a horrible second he couldn't breathe.

The boar gave a single, awful lurch. Then another. Its legs folded. It slumped forward with a grunt that sounded almost human.

Ryan whooped, already slinging the rifle back onto his shoulder. "Hell yeah! Gotcha, you fat bastard!"

Nate staggered back, face pale. "Jesus Christ," he muttered. His hands trembled as he wiped his arm against his pants, smearing blood into the fabric. He reached for his face, fingers dragging across his cheek with something close to revulsion. "What the hell is wrong with you, Ryan?"

He backed away farther, one step, then another. The image of the dying animal burned behind his eyes. The noise. The spatter. The sheer intimacy of that death. He couldn't shake it. Couldn't wipe it off.

Ryan snorted, the sound wet and full of amusement, as if the sharp crack of the rifle had lit something wild inside him. «What, you shit yourself, Nate?»

He gave another mocking snort and reached over to slap Dale's shoulder, laughter spilling out like steam from a cracked pipe. Dale, caught somewhere between discomfort and the need to belong, barked out a laugh of his own— too loud, too forced.

«That thing looked at me like I just stole its wallet,» Dale said with a grin that didn't quite reach his eyes. He laughed again, nervously this time, and Ryan cackled beside him.

Jesse stood nearby, arms crossed over his chest. He raised an eyebrow but said nothing, his face unreadable. There was no judgment in his eyes, but no amusement either. Just silence, like he was watching a movie he'd already seen and didn't particularly like.

Ryan was already pulling his phone out, angling it for the best shot. The camera shutter clicked. Once. Twice. Then again, the artificial snap of modern memory preservation echoing through the quiet woods. Without missing a beat, he planted one boot squarely on the boar's bloodied head like it was some kind of safari prize.

Nate felt something inside him twitch. He looked away, but it didn't help. The image was already printed behind his eyelids.

Dale gestured. «Hey, guys! Come on in, group photo! For the memories, huh?»

His voice was a little too high, a little too eager, like he was hoping that being part of the photo might steady whatever unease was gnawing at him. Pale and jittery, he tried to smile.

Nate didn't move. He just shook his head, muttering something under his breath, like the act of denial might scrub the scene from his mind. He rubbed at the blood on his sleeve again, hard now, as if trying to erase the texture of what had just happened.

Tyler had watched the whole thing from a few paces off, arms at his sides, unmoving. When Nate met his gaze, Tyler gave a small, crooked smile— not mocking, not amused, but laced with something quieter. Something that might've been sympathy.

He stepped closer. Nate was still wiping, his hands shaking slightly.

«I told you,» Tyler murmured. «The forest and blood... they always come together. Out here, blood's just part of the rhythm. Don't take it too hard.»

He lit a cigarette with a flick, exhaled slowly. «And keep that soft shit to yourself. Out here, it'll get you killed.»

Nate snapped his head up, eyes flashing.

«Jesus, Tyler, it's not about being soft. Enough with the damn campfire legends and whatever the hell you think this is.»

He turned toward Ryan, who was now crouched down next to the boar, adjusting the carcass for a better angle.

"This? You think this is some kind of trial? Some sick trophy hunt? No, man—this is wrong. Twisted. It's not brave, it's not tough—it's disgusting."

His voice caught, rising sharp and raw, like it scraped its way out of his throat. He ran a hand down his face, fingers trembling, then shook his head hard, as if trying to fling off whatever was crawling under his skin. The image stuck anyway—too loud, too close, too much.

He pointed a shaking hand toward the lifeless animal. «You all can call it weakness, fine. But it's wrong. This whole thing is wrong.»

Tyler didn't flinch. He took another drag from his cigarette, looking at Nate like he was trying to decide whether or not to say something more.

«It's not weakness, you know,» he said, voice calm, almost distant. «It's instinct. And instincts? They don't lie out here. You feel something's wrong? It probably is.»

The silence that followed wasn't awkward—it was heavy. Like the forest itself had paused to listen.

Nate brushed at his jacket again, a nervous tic he wasn't even aware of— smearing instead of cleaning, dragging the dark blotches of blood further into the fabric. The stain clung like memory, refusing to lift. His fingers trembled slightly, though he kept his shoulders stiff, like holding himself together physically might somehow fix the rupture in his chest.

Behind him, Ryan drove the knife deep into the boar's belly. A sickening sound followed—wet and thick, like a boot sinking into spoiled fruit. Something gave way with a squelch, and a second later came the high, elastic peel of flesh being pulled from bone.

The noise clawed at Nate's ears. His vision swam.

Voices blurred together into a low, distorted hum—like he was underwater, surrounded by laughter without faces. The trees tilted. Shadows bled at the edges of his sight, and the whole world shifted slightly off axis.

His hands fumbled for a cigarette. The first one dropped. The second he managed to light, his thumb flicking the wheel too hard. He inhaled as though it might tether him to the earth.

It didn't help.

The smell was everywhere now. Not just blood—something deeper. Older. A coppery rot that rose like steam from the gore. It invaded his throat, his lungs, his memory. It wasn't just the boar. It was the past.

"C'mon, man! This is how real men do it!" Ryan's voice broke through the haze—bright, grating, followed by sharp barks of laughter. A few chuckles rippled behind it like stones skipping on dead water.

Nate turned and walked away, unsteady. His boots slipped in the mud and blood-slick earth, nearly giving under him. His legs felt too long and too weak at once, like borrowed limbs. He staggered into the trees, catching himself against the rough bark of a pine, fingers splayed wide like a man gripping the edge of the world.

He drew in a breath—and nearly gagged.

The iron stink was here too. It lived in the back of his sinuses now. Every breath scraped.

He only made it twenty feet before his body gave up. His stomach twisted violently and bile surged up. He bent double, retching hard into the roots of the pine, the acidic burn scraping his throat raw. His whole body spasmed once, then again. He barely registered the heat of tears pricking his eyes.

Behind him, voices. Not laughter—*something messier.*

Dale let out a sharp, broken sound—half-laugh, half-yelp—like he didn't know which emotion to choose.

Ryan barked something that might've been a joke, clapped once, blood glistening on his palm. There was a wild gleam in his eyes, the kind that didn't come from joy, but from momentum. From the high of doing, not thinking.

Tyler made a sound—not quite a laugh. More like the dry exhale of someone who'd seen too much to flinch anymore. It scraped the edge of the air like wind across a tombstone.

And somehow, all of it folded into one pulsing, indistinct rhythm. It carried through the trees like smoke, reaching Nate's ears though they were far enough to be forgotten.

The sound didn't just reach him—it sank. Crawled beneath his skin. Settled in his spine.

Nate shivered, jaw tight, as if the noise itself had teeth.

He wiped his mouth with the back of his hand, heart pounding, head still low. The trees swayed around him, slow and dizzy, and the light through the branches pulsed as if through water. He pressed his forehead to the bark and just breathed. Tried to. But it came ragged, shallow. His hands wouldn't stop shaking.

The smell wouldn't leave.

He shut his eyes.

And there it was.

His father's voice—clear, close, like breath against his ear.

"You're not a hunter till you know what it feels like to be prey."

Then—

A flash.

Fog in the trees. Morning cold.

Nate, small. Rifle too big. Fingers stiff around the grip.

He remembered the weight of it. How it dragged down his arms. How his breath had fogged the air in tiny, nervous bursts. The silence around him had felt too large. Every shadow a threat. Every twig a gunshot.

Then—

The pull of the trigger.

The recoil.

The scream.

Hot blood sprayed across his face. He remembered the heat of it. The smell. How red looked black when it hit skin.

Nate jolted back into the present like surfacing from deep water. His breath came in sharp gasps, chest tight. He gripped the tree harder, like it might anchor him.

But reality wasn't better.

It was just as soaked in blood.

Ryan stood over the carcass, quiet now.

He didn't speak. Didn't gloat.

He just stared at the open belly, eyes fixed like he was trying to read something in the steam rising from the guts. His knife moved slow, careful—not out of mercy, but with a precision that was almost reverent.

Blood soaked his jeans to the knees, streaked his arms in dark, drying smears. But he didn't wipe it off. He barely seemed to notice it.

There was something in his stillness that unnerved Nate more than the laughter had. Something too calm. Too comfortable.

Ryan didn't look like a man who had just killed something.

He looked more alive than Nate had ever seen him.

Tyler's voice cut through the scene like a blade.

"Alright, boys," he said, voice gravelly and low. "Let's move. Still got ground to cover."

They moved forward as one, boots crunching over soft ground and twigs snapping like old bones beneath their weight. Shapes blurred ahead of Nate— shoulders, backs, branches, shadows. He followed, but not fully—his body moved, yes, but something behind his eyes lagged, reluctant.

For a brief moment, Jesse stood still.

He glanced back.

Their eyes met.

No judgment there. But no comfort either. Only a worn-out kind of silence—

something dulled by time and burden. Jesse's face didn't change, but there was a tightness to it, a line between the brows that hadn't been there before. He gave a shallow nod—barely perceptible.

Nate didn't know how to read it.

It wasn't encouragement. It wasn't disapproval. It just was.

Maybe that's what made it worse.

He trailed behind the others, his legs uncertain, his boots catching on roots and loose stones. The hike grew harder, the terrain more twisted—thickets thick as fists, bramble that tugged at the cuffs of their jeans like fingers trying to hold them back. The path was no path at all—just the faded ghost of old footsteps swallowed by moss.

Then, without warning, the trees fell away.

A clearing opened before them—quiet, still, touched by late light the color of old gold. It wasn't dramatic. No sacred monument. No echoing reverence. Just space. Just stillness.

And something in that stillness hummed with memory.

Jesse stopped.

"This is it," he said. "He used to hunt here. Our dad."

Jesse stood at the edge of the clearing, his arms crossed, eyes scanning the trees.

He looked like he wanted to say something—but didn't.

Nate stepped closer, waiting. Silence stretched.

Finally, Jesse exhaled, not looking at him.

"He used to bring us out here," he said. "Dad. Thought if we saw enough blood early, we'd learn not to flinch."

A pause.

"Didn't work. Not for you. Not for me either. I just got better at pretending."

The others slowed, took it in with the vacant reverence of tired men.

No one said anything else.

Somewhere behind the trees, the light slipped away.

It happened slowly, then all at once—colors draining from bark and moss until everything turned the same shade of almost-black.

A chill set in. Not the kind you notice at first, but the kind that builds in the gaps between words.

By the time they made camp, the forest was already deep in its silence. And the dark felt permanent.

Nate couldn't sleep.

Not really.

His body lay still in the tent, but his mind wouldn't follow. Images pulsed behind his eyes—flashes of torn hide, of blood steaming in the air, of laughter twisted at the edges. Every time his breath slowed, something jolted him awake. Something just beneath dreaming.

There's no such thing as a bloodless forest... You bleed, or you take blood. That's the deal. That's always been the deal.

Tyler's voice echoed in his skull like it had been carved there.

Nate shuddered.

Every time he closed his eyes, it was there again: the moose. Its body flayed, hollowed. Empty eye sockets like black wells. Feathers trembling in bloody grass. Then the gunshot—Ryan's voice, the death-writhing of the boar. Blood on his hands. On his face. Still warm. Still clinging.

He jolted upright in his tent, lungs snapping open like a drowning man's. Cold sweat clung to his skin. His chest heaved.

Then—

A sound.

Branches shifting.

A cry.

Raw. Violent. Not human.

Nate scrambled to his feet, stumbling over the sleeping bag as he threw himself toward the flap. He pushed it aside, stepping into the freezing dark.

The forest didn't move—but something had.

The air felt carved from stone. The trees looked wrong. Off. He scanned the clearing—

—and saw it.

Lying in the dirt, just beyond the tent line.

A bracelet. Bone-white. Strung with cord and weathered beads.

Tyler's.

Nate moved toward it, each step slower than the last. He knelt, trembling fingers reaching down, brushing the earth as he picked it up. The weight of it was light, but in his palm it felt heavy as guilt.

"Tyler?" he called softly, barely trusting his own voice. "Tyler!"

No answer.

The branches overhead shifted again. No wind. No reason. Just motion.

Behind him—footsteps. Fast. Panicked.

Ryan burst from his tent, rifle in hand, followed by Jesse and Dale stumbling after him.

"Hey! What the hell's going on?" Ryan barked, eyes sharp and unfocused, the barrel of the gun swinging too fast.

Nate turned, still clutching the bracelet. His breath came in clouds.

Dale, pale and wide-eyed, pointed. "I—I heard him. He was walking out here. Then he screamed…"

Jesse stormed toward Nate, his face tight.

"What the hell happened?" Jesse growled, stopping just short of him. "Did you see something?"

Nate shook his head, slowly—like every motion had weight.

"No…" he said, the word catching in his throat. "I heard a scream. Then I found this…"

He looked down again at the bracelet in his palm—Tyler's bone beads, dulled by time, now streaked faintly with damp earth. It looked too still. Too placed.

His voice dropped to a whisper.

"I think… I think something happened to him."

The others fell silent.

Somewhere beyond the circle of tents, the forest watched.

Jesse stepped forward, eyes scanning the trees. Ryan muttered something and raised his rifle, but didn't aim it—just held it like a charm against something he couldn't name.

The dirt beneath their feet was disturbed where Tyler had last stood. Boot prints. Scuffed leaves. Broken twigs.

And then—nothing.

The tracks just stopped.

No continuation. No drag marks. No turn.

Like he'd been lifted out of the world.

Nate stared into the dark. Past the reach of flashlights. Past the trees and into the spaces between them. Where the black was too black. Where sound didn't echo. Where air didn't move.

And he felt it.

Not wind. Not cold.

Something deeper.

Like breath—low, wide, ancient. And beneath it, a pulse.

Not his.

Not human.

The forest was awake now.

And it was listening.

A chill crawled across the back of his neck, ran the length of his spine in a line of pins and needles. The kind of cold that doesn't come from temperature—but from recognition. From something staring back.

His skin prickled. His hands clenched without realizing it.

Something was in that darkness.

Not watching.

Hunting.

He couldn't explain how he knew. But he did. The way animals know before storms. The way silence feels wrong before it breaks.

He turned slowly, scanning the trees—looking for movement, for eyeshine, for anything.

But the woods gave nothing back.

Only the sense that they had *shifted*—invisible angles bending, sounds muffled just enough to feel wrong.

Tonight... something else was moving.

And whatever it was—

—it had just stepped inside the circle.

Chapter 4:

Tusks and Blood

The trees still bled by morning.

Time had lost its shape. It moved in uneven waves, dragging panic in its wake. The forest felt like it was buzzing—not with life, but with dread, like every leaf was rattling with it. Not a rustle, not a breeze. A tremor. A frequency. It vibrated somewhere beneath the skin, like a drill boring straight into bone.

There was no morning freshness, no bite of cool air to wake the senses. Just a heavy, suffocating damp that clung to the lungs like wet wool. And the stains—they were still there.

Dark, tacky blotches streaked tree trunks and soaked into the moss below, blackened at the edges, already crusting. It looked less like blood and more like the forest had hemorrhaged in the night. Like something in it had died— and kept dying.

No one questioned what it was. No one needed to.

Nate smoked. He didn't know how many he'd gone through—didn't care. His fingers trembled with each drag, clinging to the cigarette like it might tether him to reality. His jaw ached from clenching. His thoughts spun with no direction, a carousel of static and noise. No plans, no next step. Just the cigarette. Just not screaming.

"Shit, I don't get it," Ryan snapped. He paced, erratic, hands flexing at his sides like he was looking for something to punch. His nerves never showed like other people's—they didn't shake. They boiled. "Something pulled him. Something pulled him. But what the hell pulls a man? With a gun? Tyler had a damn gun."

Jesse stood over a wide smear on the ground, jaw locked so tight it could snap. His fingers drummed once against the barrel of his rifle. He kept glancing sideways into the trees, like expecting Tyler to step out from between them. Or worse, something else.

His voice came low and flat.

"Nothing. There's nothing out here that could've done this."

The pause that followed said he didn't believe his own words.

Dale just stood off to the side, wide-eyed and pale. Like the forest had changed shape while they slept. Like the trees weren't quite in the same place anymore.

"Maybe… maybe we try again," he offered, voice too high. He gestured toward the thicker brush, where the branches curled like fingers.

Nobody moved.

Nate dragged again, lips tightening around the filter. The smoke burned going in, but it was the only thing keeping his hands from shaking worse. The cigarette trembled anyway. The stains didn't dry. And the forest wouldn't stop watching.

Jesse's voice cut through the damp silence.

"We were just there."

Dale hesitated, rubbing the back of his neck, his voice barely louder than a whisper. "I mean… maybe we go a little farther. Just a bit."

He looked around, eyes pleading not to be laughed at. For once, he wasn't cracking a joke, wasn't trying to follow—he was trying to lead. There was a flicker of something real in his voice. Maybe courage. Maybe guilt.

Ryan turned on him like a whip.

"You damn idiot," he snarled, jabbing a finger toward the ground. "Did you see this?!"

Blood smeared the grass like paint strokes from something blind and angry.

"Why are you even talking? Who said anyone wants to hear you?"

Jesse stepped between them before it could escalate, but his eyes were hard.

"What could've done this?" he asked, more to himself than anyone. "What takes a man like that—without a trace?"

Ryan paced in a short, savage line, like a dog too long on a chain.

"Hell if I know," he muttered. "But not Tyler. No way. If it was Dale, or Nate? Sure. But Tyler?" He spat, glaring into the maze of trees. "He knew these woods. He had the rifle."

Nate spoke quietly, but the words cut through the clearing like a blade.

"We need to go back."

The others froze. Turned. Stared.

"What?" Nate said, lifting the bracelet in his fingers, its bone beads catching the weak morning light. "We heard the scream. Then we found this. Then... that."

He didn't need to point again. The smear said everything.

"You really think he's okay?"

Ryan snorted.

"Oh good, the expert speaks again."

"Tyler's not coming back," Nate said, steady now. "Something happened to him. And we need to get the hell out of here while we still can. Call the cops. Let someone else find whatever the hell this is."

Ryan glared at him, fury twitching just beneath his skin. For a second, Nate couldn't tell if he was about to explode—on him, on Dale, on the forest itself. There was something unhinged in his eyes, something animal. But then Ryan just held the stare, jaw tight, and gave the smallest, most reluctant nod. Like it scraped something raw inside him to admit Nate was right.

Then—a sound.

A groan, long and low. Somewhere between a creaking tree and a growl. It rolled through the woods like thunder beneath the soil.

All of them turned.

Nate's heart slammed into his ribs. His fingers tightened involuntarily around the bracelet. The trees looked the same. And yet... not. The bark seemed sharper. The shadows deeper. As if the forest had grown teeth overnight.

Ryan let out a short grunt, turned on his heel, and started walking.

Dale followed quick behind, almost tripping over a root. Jesse waited half a second, then exhaled and turned too.

Nate lingered, still staring into the place the sound had come from. It still echoed faintly, like a whisper dragged through gravel. Something cold moved through his chest.

"Hey," Jesse called softly. A hand on Nate's shoulder. "Let's go."

They moved forward.

Ryan led. His boots cracked the underbrush like bones. There was a weight to him, something coiled and dangerous in the way he moved—like he wasn't walking, but hunting. Every step radiated that same cold aggression, the kind that didn't bark or shout—it just crushed. Nate watched him for a long moment. That kind of strength didn't build things. It broke them.

The trees blurred past as they moved—but the path wasn't the same.

What should've been a clear trail through thinning woods had twisted into a mess of bramble and roots that looked like they had clawed up from beneath the soil overnight. The trees leaned in, shoulder to shoulder, crowding out the sky. Light pierced through in broken shafts, flickering like something wounded. Time itself felt wrong—moving too fast and too slow at once. The air hung thick, damp, like something had already breathed it all in.

Everything had changed.

The path curved in ways Nate didn't remember. And the trees—he could swear they'd grown closer together.

His thoughts were a blur. Just keeping it together was work now. Blood kept flashing in his mind—dark, thick, impossible to forget. In his pocket, his fingers clutched the bracelet like a talisman, bone beads digging into his skin. Tyler wasn't alive. He didn't know how he knew it, but he did. And that knowledge sat inside him like ice.

He didn't want to remember, didn't mean to—but the memory pushed forward anyway.

The blood. The moose, its eyes gone. The black crows, wings outstretched, one twitching in the wind. Then the sound—the high, dying scream of the boar and the wet rip of flesh splitting beneath a knife. And the smell.

Nate flinched, face tightening.

His thoughts started to spiral again—but something caught his eye.

Movement.

Fast. Fluid. Wrong.

Not close. Not clear. A shadow—large, low, moving through the trees like water. Like oil slicking through bark. Nate froze.

It wasn't clear, but he saw it. Just a glimpse, but long enough to know it stopped. For a heartbeat, it stopped. And it looked at him.

Eyes. Too high off the ground.

Not just seen—felt. The gaze stabbed through him like a blade of ice. It was watching him in a way that didn't belong in the world. Not curiosity. Not hunger. Something older.

Then the weight dropped.

Like the sky had suddenly crashed down. Nate's knees wobbled under invisible pressure. No wind. No birds. No insects. Just silence. Just his breath.

He staggered and squinted, trying to lock on the spot. But it was gone. Nothing but still trees. Too still. As if the whole forest was holding its breath. And inside him, something crawled—cold, slow tendrils wrapping his chest.

"Hey," Jesse's voice cut through from beside him. "You okay?"

"No," Nate said quickly. He backed up a step, still staring. "I told you," he hissed. "I told you this was a bad idea."

"Oh, don't start," Jesse snapped, irritated. "Now's not the time—"

"No." Nate turned on him, louder than he meant, jabbing a finger toward Jesse's chest. "You never listen. You dragged us out here to chase ghosts and pretend it was about Dad. But it's not. This is about you. And look where we are now."

Jesse's face darkened. His voice rose with equal heat. "Oh, give me a break. You think this is my fault?"

"Yes!" Nate roared.

And the forest, somehow, felt quieter still.

Jesse narrowed his eyes, sharp and unforgiving. "Everything's a mess, huh? Then maybe you should've stayed in the city, shuffling papers in your cozy little office. What the hell are you even doing here, Nate?"

"I've been asking myself that same damn question," Nate muttered, eyes flat.

Jesse's expression twisted—not angry, not exactly. More like disappointment coiled tight. "You know, I thought... I thought maybe you felt it too. That ache. That weight in your chest when you think about Dad. I thought this would mean something. That maybe it would pull us back together." He shook his head, bitter. "I figured some part of you still belonged to this family. I guess I was wrong. You'd rather wallow in your own damn misery. Drown in it. Maybe it's safer for you that way. Staying broken means you never have to move forward."

"Shut up, Jess." Nate's voice cracked, not weak but raw. His eyes were wide now, lit with something dangerous. "You hear me? Just shut the hell up. You always turn it into this. Always digging up the past. Like we don't have anything else to talk about. A man's gone—probably dead—and you're still stuck on what happened to me, not even to you. Let it go."

"Oh, boys," came Ryan's voice, too close, slithering in from somewhere behind. "Are we doing therapy now?"

Nate turned, startled. Ryan stood behind him, arms folded, face twisted in a sneer. "What is it this time? Our little princess crying again?"

"Screw off, Ryan," Nate snapped.

Ryan didn't flinch. Instead, he stepped forward, his breath hot, eyes wild and edged. "You know what?" he growled. "I'm not in the damn mood for your soap opera. So take your whiny crap and shove it. We've got bigger problems."

"I said—screw off," Nate barked back, shoving Ryan hard in the chest. "Don't tell me what to say."

Jesse reached out, palm raised. "Stop. Come on, both of you. Just—calm down."

Dale winced. "He's kinda right, Nate. This isn't helping. No one wants to hear all your drama right now."

He glanced at Ryan, like a kid checking if he'd said the right thing in front of the loudest voice in the room.

"Get off me," Nate hissed, yanking his arm away from Jesse's grip. "All of you—just back the hell off!" The words burst out sharper than he expected, and even he looked startled by his own voice.

"Nate—" Jesse started.

"And you too, Jess." Nate's finger pointed like a blade. "Don't come any closer."

Ryan snorted—not loud, but sharp. Then he grabbed Nate by the shoulder, fingers digging in. "Back off? Or what?"

The air thickened again.

And something deeper than anger flared behind Nate's eyes.

Something old.

Something ready to break.

Nate shoved Ryan again, this time harder, chest rising and falling like a storm barely held in place. His hands trembled—fists clenched so tightly his knuckles had gone white. Something snapped inside him. Not a thought. Not even rage. Just that primal, seething jolt of energy that erupts when the line is finally crossed. And there was no reeling it back in.

Ryan's face flared with the same wild fire, lips curled, eyes feral. He didn't wait. He didn't hesitate. There was something almost gleeful in the way he lunged—like he'd been waiting for this.

To Nate, it happened in a blink. A blur. A flash.

And then—**impact.**

Ryan's fist cracked into the side of his head. Nate didn't even register the blow before the ground rose to meet him. His back slammed into a root, pain flowering sharp across his spine. His nose exploded in heat, blood gushing down his lip and over his chin. He gasped, chest hitching, mouth full of copper.

"You flap your mouth like a man," Ryan said, towering over him, his voice a venomous sneer, "but fall like a sack of bones." He squinted down, almost amused. Then he spit into the dirt beside Nate's head. «All noise. That's all you are.»

"Hey! Enough!" Jesse rushed forward, crouching beside Nate, hands out like a referee. "Ryan, seriously. Not now."

His voice faltered, scattered. He wasn't even sure what he was saying anymore—just trying to defuse a bomb with a whisper.

Nate groaned, wiping blood from his upper lip. It smeared red across the back of his hand. He sniffed, a thick, wet sound, then looked down at the mess streaked across his skin.

"Shit," he muttered, more to himself than anyone else. He swatted Jesse's hand away and sat up slowly, ribs aching.

Still breathing hard, Nate locked eyes with Ryan. That look—cold, hard, bull-like—stayed locked on him. Ryan didn't move. Didn't blink. Just stared, like sizing up a wounded animal.

And the forest felt... bent. Skewed. Like the tension between them had warped the very air.

"Guys..." Dale's voice came again, strained. "Uh... guys?"

The words snapped like a twig.

Heavy drops began to fall. Rain. Not gentle. Not forgiving. It came fast and fat, splattering against skin and leaves like stones.

Nate flinched, one drop hitting the bridge of his broken nose. He hissed, blinking through the sting.

"Guys, seriously—come here," Dale said again, now breathless. "I think..."

Everyone turned.

The air had changed.

It was *colder.*

The trees seemed bent inward, their shapes wrong. From somewhere just beyond them came a sound—a crunch. Wet. Deliberate. Like something stepped not on wood, but on meat.

Dale let out a choked yelp and scrambled back.

Jesse reached him first—and stopped cold.

Ryan caught up next. He didn't say anything. Just stood there, mouth slightly open.

Nate pushed to his feet, wincing. Blood still flowed, warm and thick. He swayed slightly as he moved closer, drawn by the silence. He looked at their faces—Jesse pale, Dale trembling—then followed their eyes down.

Something red lay in the grass.

Closer.

His stomach twisted.

A hand.

Severed at the wrist, the fingers curled in a dead man's spasm, nails black with soil.

A little further—an arm.

A torso.

A ribcage, peeled half open.

Not arranged. Not buried.

Scattered.

As if something had torn it apart and left the pieces behind like a game.

Nate stared, frozen, unable to drag his eyes away. The world spun. His stomach twisted violently, a sick heat crawling up the back of his throat. He knew this feeling—this particular, spiraling dread. It wasn't new. It had begun days ago, when they saw the moose. When the crows circled. When the blood painted the leaves. This... this was just the crescendo. A nightmare with no seams.

Beside him, Jesse clenched his jaw so tight the muscles rippled beneath his skin. Ryan had gone pale, not out of fear, but something colder. Dale backed into a tree, visibly shaking, his breath coming in erratic bursts.

The trail continued forward—a long, wet smear.

Tyler.

Or what was left of him.

Chunks. Shreds. Ribbons of flesh and fabric littered the moss like some butchered puzzle. Rain drummed against the carnage, thick drops striking with grotesque rhythm. The pieces weren't placed. They were scattered, thrown—like something had played with them.

Nate stepped back. His spine pressed against the bark of a tree, fingers clawing into the wet trunk as if it could anchor him to the world. He shut his eyes, but the images pulsed behind the lids. A severed hand. A ribcage. A boot with nothing inside it.

Jesse moved forward, slowly, like someone wading into dark water. His lips parted but no words came. Only a faint tremor in his mouth, a betrayal of his composure. Then finally, quietly:

«No.»

Ryan crouched by the remains, his gaze analytical, cold. Like a hunter assessing a kill. He scanned the forest, nostrils flaring slightly. Rain dripped from his lashes, his jaw set in grim calculation.

«Jesus Christ,» Jesse breathed. «What the hell did this?»

Dale shook his head rapidly, voice trembling. «W-what if it's still hunting? What if it's not done?»

«Shut it,» Ryan snapped. His eyes narrowed at the mangled tissue. He lowered himself closer, his face inches from a ragged hunk of muscle. Nate gagged.

Ryan didn't blink. «Not teeth.»

Jesse turned sharply. «What?»

Ryan looked up at them, rain dripping down his temples.

«These marks. Not teeth. Something else. Something worse.»

He stood abruptly, lit a cigarette with trembling fingers. The flame hissed in the damp air. Smoke coiled above Tyler's remains. Ryan stared deep into the trees, eyes distant.

And then—

A sound.

Too fast. Too raw. A shriek? A growl?

Nate couldn't name it.

Movement.

Dark. Blurred. It came like a ripple of fury through the trees.

Dale never had a chance.

Something massive barreled from the underbrush, a blur of fur and muscle, rage incarnate. It struck Dale like a truck, lifting him off the ground, dragging him screaming into the shadows. His body disappeared into a wall of green and brown.

«Dale!» Jesse shouted, surging forward.

They all ran.

Branches whipped Nate's face, the rain now a pounding fury. He ran, chest heaving, legs burning. Pain lanced through his shoulder with every stride. He couldn't keep up.

Jesse was ahead. Then Ryan.

Leaves slapped at Nate's cheeks. His lungs clawed for air. The shadows thickened, branches grabbing at his clothes like hands. The rain roared now, blinding, hammering down through the canopy.

Nate stopped just behind Jesse, his boots skidding to a halt in the wet underbrush.

Jesse was already kneeling beside Dale, doing something with his jacket—pressing down hard, trying to slow the bleeding. Rain streaked Jesse's back, soaking his flannel and hair, but he didn't seem to notice. His hands worked fast, but his breath was ragged. Nate noticed how his fingers trembled around the fabric, how his jaw clenched so tight a muscle jumped near his temple.

There was something else, too—just a flicker. Jesse's eyes glistened, and he blinked hard, like forcing back tears was the only way to keep moving.

Ryan stood a few feet away, rifle raised, scanning the shadows. His chest heaved, nostrils flaring with every breath. The trees loomed tighter around them now, thick with mist and something else—something heavier.

Nate stepped forward, blinking through the downpour. Dale's face was pale, lips slick with blood. His shirt was soaked red from shoulder to waist, clinging to the torn flesh beneath.

Deep, ragged wounds tore across his side—wide and uneven, as if something had ripped through flesh with brute force but no precision. Not claw marks exactly. Not anything Nate could name. Just raw violence, carved into Dale's body in thick, open slashes. Blood soaked through the torn fabric, heavy and dark, pooling beneath him in slow, deliberate pulses.

The sight made Nate's stomach flip. His head swam, light and dizzy. He pressed a hand to a nearby trunk, grounding himself. The bark felt too cold, too rough, like it didn't belong to the world he'd known before this moment.

"What the hell was that?" Nate said, voice hoarse. He stumbled forward another step. "Dale? What the hell was that thing?"

Dale choked on a cough, blood spilling over his bottom lip. His eyes fluttered open, clouded, unfocused. For a second, Nate wasn't even sure he could speak.

"It was—" Dale coughed again, weaker this time. "It was big... huge. I think—I think it was a boar. But not really."

His voice cracked, then trailed off. He blinked slowly, as if it took all his strength just to keep his gaze on Nate.

"It was a monster," Dale whispered.

The words cut through the rain like a blade.

Jesse looked up at Nate, eyes wide, jaw clenched tight with helplessness. Ryan still hadn't lowered his weapon. Around them, the forest seemed to hold its breath.

Somewhere beyond the trees, something moved.

And the blood kept coming.

Chapter 5:
Echoes of the Hunt

The forest dripped.

From every branch, every fern, every ragged strip of moss, rain gathered and slid off in thick, deliberate drops. It wasn't a downpour—no sheets of silver flash—but a slow, relentless seep, the kind of rain that didn't fall so much as it *clung*. The air was swollen with it, pressing close, fogging breath, hanging like a wet cloth over skin and spirit. The smell wasn't the crisp scent of clean rain on dry leaves. It was sour. Stale. A rot that had learned how to breathe. The forest didn't smell like life anymore.

The fire sputtered in the clearing like a dying animal, flames curling inward, as though retreating from the damp. It hissed when a fat drop struck its heart, recoiled like something wounded. What little heat it gave off barely reached the boots of the men huddled around it. Not that it mattered.

Dale lay curled beneath a tarp fashioned from his poncho and the remains of a shredded thermal blanket. His face had gone pale hours ago—but now it was something else entirely. A gray-green hue had crept into his skin, like the color of deep water, with dark bruising blooming beneath his eyes. His lips were cracked and dry, despite the damp, and when his eyes opened briefly, the color seemed to have drained from them too—duller, emptier.

His chest rose and fell in shaky, irregular pulls. The crude bandage wrapped around his thigh had darkened again, soaked through by something that smelled too much like metal. But that wasn't the worst of it. His side—ripped open by whatever had struck him—was swathed in a tattered cloth, cinched tight, but the wound beneath pulsed faintly with each heartbeat, leaking something dark and sticky.

Rain tapped at the edge of his makeshift shelter and splattered across his forehead. He didn't flinch. Didn't blink. But then he made a sound—low at first. Wet. Gurgling.

Nate startled.

The voice rose, muttering, incoherent, but shaped like language. Words never fully formed—but some did. Some came out louder than others. And those moments were the worst. Because when Dale's voice rose above a whisper, it wasn't just the volume—it was the tone.

It was a voice that didn't sound like it belonged to Dale anymore. It sounded borrowed. Wrenched out from some black throat buried miles below their feet. Ragged and hoarse, full of panic and pain.

"Behind... it's *behind*... it sees..."

Nate had leapt up the first time Dale had screamed like that. The way his voice cut through the quiet made his skin crawl. It made the trees lean in. Every time it happened, Nate's heart punched hard into his ribs and his stomach clenched so fast it hurt. Dale's cries weren't just the fever talking. They felt like truth.

And that was the worst part.

The fire snapped again. Another drop hissed into the coals. Nate sat, elbows on his knees, fingers trembling near his mouth. The cigarette between them had long since burned out. He hadn't noticed. He wasn't cold, though he should've been. He wasn't hungry, though his stomach had been empty for hours.

All he could feel was pressure. Thought, smashed together. Like his brain couldn't find a straight line, only circles. Thought loops that led nowhere.

What pulled Dale?

What was strong enough to do that?

What was fast enough?

What was it?

The moment played in his head over and over again. Dale being yanked into the dark like a sack of meat. The snapping branches. The scream. The dragging. And then the silence.

Every time he tried to remember it clearly, to name it, to define it—fear closed over him like a jaw. A cold, iron clamp around his lungs. Like even the idea of the thing was off-limits.

His chest burned. His hands shook. There was a tightness at the base of his throat, a creeping nausea in the pit of his stomach. Every time Dale spoke, every time that low, awful voice slipped from under the tarp, it was like a match tossed into the oil drum inside Nate's ribs.

The words echoed.

Monster... it was a monster...

They circled in Nate's mind like flies over something spoiled, relentless and foul. Again and again, the thought pierced through the fog—no bear, no moose, no half-remembered nightmare. A monster.

He looked again at Dale—the limp, twitching form beneath the sagging tarp. A shoulder jerked. A foot spasmed. With each fragile motion, fresh blood oozed from the soaked bandages on his thigh and side, dripping into the blackened earth. The ground accepted it without complaint.

Nate sat close, knees pulled tight to his chest, the cigarette between his fingers nothing but a quivering ember. Smoke curled upward and vanished into the damp night. He couldn't stop watching Dale—afraid that if he looked away, he might disappear. Or worse, change. Like sheer focus could anchor him to what was left of his humanity.

"He's getting worse," Jesse murmured, squatting beside Dale with muddy hands and tired eyes. His voice came soft, almost too soft to hear over the whispering rain. It was the kind of voice that didn't want to disturb something fragile—or already broken.

From the edge of the clearing came the guttural sound of Ryan tipping another bottle skyward—probably not his first. He grunted loudly, a sound halfway between a belch and a growl, then wiped his mouth with the back of his hand. The rifle lay across his lap like an extension of his rage, his knuckles clenched around the grip. He wasn't drunk. He didn't get drunk.

He was coiled. Watchful. Like something waiting to strike.

His eyes, bloodshot and too bright, burned toward the trees. There was something in his posture—head tilted slightly, jaw clenched—that suggested he expected the forest itself to step out and challenge him. And if it did, he would tear it apart with his teeth if the bullets ran out.

For a moment, Nate looked at him. Ryan caught the glance and offered a crooked grin—one that belonged more to a predator than a man.

Nate said nothing. His jaw tightened until pain bloomed at the hinge, then he turned away, rubbing the back of his neck, fingers kneading tense muscle. His nose still pulsed from the earlier punch, a deep ache that flared with every breath. He sniffed, sharp and dry, then wiped beneath one eye with the heel of his hand.

His head pounded. Not pain exactly—more like pressure. Like something inside his skull was trying to get out. He looked toward the woods again, just beyond the reach of the fire's flickering light. The trees stood like statues, coated in black moss, limbs curling downward like broken fingers. They didn't sway. Didn't move. But they watched. He could feel it.

Jesse followed his gaze. They sat like that for a long while, not speaking. Just breathing. Listening.

The forest whispered.

Not loudly. Not in words. But in the language of things too old to translate. The way the rain hit the leaves. The way it slid down trunks and disappeared into root and loam. The way every drop felt like it had purpose.

Nate leaned in closer to the fire.

"What the hell was that?" he whispered. "What did that to Dale?"

Jesse flinched. Just slightly. His face tensed, and his brow furrowed like he was trying not to remember something he'd already seen too clearly.

"I don't know," Jesse said. "You saw it too. Something... off. But what the hell was it? Boar..." He snorted, bitter. "Feels stupid even saying it now."

He stared at the flames. Rain crackled in the branches overhead.

"Absurd," he muttered. "Just... absurd."

Then, after a moment, he added, "Remember how Dad used to line up cans on the fence?"

His voice shifted—smaller now. Not just tired. Something more fragile underneath, something buried deep and left untouched for years. It quivered when it came out, like it wasn't sure if it wanted to be heard at all.

Nate smiled faintly, the corner of his mouth twitching up with something between warmth and regret. "Yeah. I remember. He talked more to his rifle than he ever did to us."

Jesse let out a dry breath that might've been a laugh in a different life. "He did. But you still loved him. We both did."

"Yeah. I did."

Nate took a long drag, the ember flaring like a dying star. Smoke trailed from his lips in a slow curl, lost quickly to the mist. "I've thought a lot about that. About all the things I never got to say. Jess... you were right earlier. I haven't moved on. That day... it keeps playing in my head. Over and over."

He stared into the fire, his voice cracking at the edges. "Hell, sometimes I see it when I blink."

He tapped his temple, fingers trembling. "If he hadn't taught me to shoot... if I hadn't picked up that damn rifle—none of it would've happened."

Jesse shook his head slowly. "You were a kid. A scared kid. It was an accident."

"I know. But that doesn't matter. Doesn't make it disappear."

His jaw trembled. "I'm still there, Jess. Every time I smell cordite. Every time I see blood. I'm still there, goddammit."

Jesse didn't speak right away. He leaned closer and placed a hand gently on Nate's shoulder—a brief, grounding pressure.

"It's okay, man," he said.

A beat.

"Really."

The silence that followed stretched long and thin, like a wire drawn taut between them. Rain ticked softly on the leaves above. And somewhere deeper in the woods, a branch creaked. Not from wind. Not from weight. Just... creaked.

Under the tarp, Dale stirred.

His hand emerged, trembling as though it carried the weight of a mountain. Fingers curled like dying leaves. His eyes fluttered open for a breath—clouded, glassy, ringed in red. But he didn't look at them. He looked through them, gaze unfocused, as if caught between worlds.

Tiny veins had burst in the whites of his eyes, turning them a pinkish hue that made the irises look ghostly, almost translucent. His skin was even paler now—chalk-white, dry as paper. And his brow shone slick with sweat.

"Shit... it's out there... it was there..." he whispered, his voice rasping like sand on stone.

Sweat rolled down from his temples as he struggled to lift his head. "Tusks..." he gasped. "I saw its tusks..."

Nate leaned forward, instinctively.

"Dale?"

"They laugh," Dale muttered, eyes drifting. "They laugh while it screams. The whole forest's awake now... it's coming back..."

His hand reached upward, fumbling at the air, grasping for something not there. His arm trembled, then dropped, limp and lifeless, like a severed rope.

But he didn't pass out.

He lay still, eyes half-closed, lips parted. Not unconscious—just gone somewhere deeper. Somewhere they couldn't follow.

Nate turned to Jesse, voice low but urgent. "You heard that, right?"

Jesse didn't answer. He just kept staring into the forest, his eyes narrowed as though trying to catch a shape in the dark. Something he wasn't sure he wanted to find.

"Jess…"

"What?"

Nate hesitated. His words came slowly, like he wasn't sure he should speak them aloud. "There's something in this forest. You know it. I know it. Dad... I think he knew it too."

Jesse gave a short nod, not looking away from the trees. "He still came out here," he said. "Still dragged us along."

"Why?" Nate whispered. "This place… it was his. If there's something out here—he couldn't not know. He knew this forest like the back of his hand."

Jesse finally turned to him, jaw tight. "Right now, I think we need to focus on how to get the hell out. We can talk philosophy later."

He faced Nate fully, too fast. His voice sharpened. "But for that to happen, Nate, you need to remember who you are."

Nate's brow lifted. "What?"

"If that thing—whatever the hell it is—ripped Tyler apart and tried to do the same to Dale," Jesse said, jabbing a finger toward Dale's convulsing silhouette under the tarp, "then it's real. It's dangerous. And it's coming back."

He locked eyes with Nate. "And if it comes back, you need to be able to protect yourself."

Jesse reached down and shoved the rifle closer to him.

"No," Nate said flatly. "I told you already."

"This isn't about want or don't want, Nate. This is survival," Jesse snapped. "Ours. Yours. If you don't pick that up, people can die. You can die."

Nate took a slow drag from his cigarette, exhaled hard through his nose, his expression hardening.

"No."

"Jess, you need to understand," he said, leaning back, voice quieter but no less firm. "I'm not like you. I don't have your strength, your belief. I'm not built for this. I used to think it was fear. But it's more than that."

"You used to shoot just like me," Jesse said. "Better, even."

"That time's gone," Nate said, cutting him off. "Long gone. So let it go. I'm not touching that thing."

Jesse threw up his hands, frustration boiling over. "That's just stupid, Nate. Are you really this dense? Goddamn."

He looked at him, eyes wide with disbelief. "I can't believe this. You're just—" He cursed under his breath, his voice thick with fury. "What the hell is wrong with you?"

"Call it what you want, Jess," Nate said, voice sharp now, each word like a slap. "But you never understood. I keep telling you and you don't hear me. You never hear me. This isn't for me. It never was. I tried to run from it—all of it."

He motioned to the shadows just beyond the firelight.

"And now all this blood… it feels like echoes. Echoes of the hunt. Of him. Of every kill. Every time we carved something open and called it a lesson."

He swept a hand toward the trees, eyes burning.

"I see that same look in your eyes he used to get—right before pulling the trigger and calling it love for nature."

Nate shot Jesse a hard look, like he didn't recognize him anymore.

"I'm not turning into that. Not again. Not for you. Not for anyone."

Jesse stared into the fire, eyes glassy with reflection. «Then be different,» he said. «But don't stand still while this thing eats us alive. Or are you just gonna sit there and watch?"

The fire cracked. Rain whispered through the canopy like breath through clenched teeth.

A shape stirred at the edge of the clearing—just a ripple of shadow at first. Then came the heavy crunch of boots. Ryan emerged from the dark, soaked to the bone and bristling with anger. A half-empty bottle swung from one fist. He slumped down by the fire with a grunt, rubbing his face hard, like he could wipe away the cold.

"You two…" he muttered with a sneer, the smell of alcohol and something fouler—dampness, sweat, rot—rolling off him in waves. "Christ. Family therapy again?"

He lit a cigarette with fingers that moved too fast, too sharp, like they were arguing with the flame. He stared into the woods like it was a rival. Not just something to be feared—something to be challenged. To be fought.

"So what've we got?" he said, exhaling smoke like steam from a pressure valve. "Tyler's gone."

His eyes flicked to Dale, who stirred weakly under the tarp.

"That one's dead on his feet and we still gotta haul his ass. Great."

He turned back to the trees and drew deep from the cigarette, the tip flaring. "This thing—whatever it is—I'm gonna find it. And I'm gonna kill it." He raised his free hand, clenching it into a massive, white-knuckled fist. "Hell, I'd tear it apart with my bare hands if I could."

Jesse glanced up. "I think we wait for daylight. Then we get the hell out of here."

Ryan snorted, but nodded once. "That's not enough. You hear me? Not enough. I don't let things cross the line with me. No one does. And this thing?" He jabbed a finger at the woods. "This thing crossed it. It challenged me. I don't let that go."

His eyes lit up with a wild fire—bright, reckless, terrifying.

"We're going to make that bastard pay," he growled. "Whatever it is—we'll find it, we'll tear it to pieces. And we'll drink its damn blood in Tyler's name."

He slammed his fist into the dirt beside him, breath heaving.

"I'm not letting this go, goddammit!" he roared, the last words tearing from his throat like a savage howl.

Nate watched him with a mix of skepticism and unease. Even in his half-sober state—no, especially in it—Ryan radiated something dark and volatile. Not drunk, not in the usual way. But overfull. Wired with something raw and hungry. A furious, animal energy hummed beneath his skin, making him twitch, shift, crack his knuckles. He couldn't sit still. Couldn't stop.

The muscles in his jaw jumped. His eyes never left the trees, as if waiting for them to step forward and offer him the fight he so badly wanted.

Nate exhaled smoke through his nose and lit another cigarette, the flame from the lighter briefly illuminating the lines etched deep around his eyes.

"Listen," he said slowly, frowning as he drew in a breath. "I've been thinking… I know how this is gonna sound, but—Tyler used to talk about something being out here. He called it The Boar That Hunts Back. The One Who Hunts Hunters. A spirit. A punishment. A reckoning in flesh. You remember that?"

Ryan and Jesse both turned to him with matching expressions—part disbelief, part mockery.

"I'm not joking," Nate said. "You all heard him. I just…"

"Jesus Christ," Ryan muttered, rolling his eyes hard enough to see his skull. He shifted in place, then leaned in, the bottle swaying at his side like a club. "What's next, cupcake? You want me to tuck you in and read you a bedtime story about forest spirits?»

"I wasn't talking to you," Nate snapped. "And I don't give a shit what you think."

Jesse rubbed the back of his neck, frowning. "Tyler did say that stuff, yeah. But…" He hesitated. "Tyler said a lot of things. He loved those stories."

"Maybe they weren't just stories," Nate said, his voice quieter now. "Every story comes from somewhere. I mean, what if—"

"Oh, for God's sake," Ryan cut in, his thick-necked bulk shifting toward Nate like a freight train angling for a collision. His eyes—red, unblinking—locked onto him with a predator's focus. "You serious right now? You gonna play forest shaman? Gonna dance around the fire next?"

But this time, Nate didn't flinch. He stared right back, squinting slightly like narrowing a scope.

"Go to hell, Ryan."

"Enough," Jesse said sharply, crouching over Dale and adjusting the blood-soaked bandages. Dale groaned under the pressure, a weak, rattling sound. "Save the macho bullshit for later—he's bleeding out. He's not gonna last another day like this."

The fire crackled loud in the pause that followed. The glow lit Ryan's face with feral angles, turning his expression into something primitive. For a moment, Nate thought something inside him had cracked. That he might launch across the fire and come for him.

But instead, to Nate's surprise, Ryan just raised his eyebrows—an expression that looked like surprise, but was probably restraint. Barely. A crooked, venomous grin curled at his lips as he took another swig from the bottle, the amber liquid sloshing.

His hand trembled. His breath came hard.

Jesse stood, wiping his blood-smeared hands on his jeans. "All right," he muttered. "I'll be right back." He jerked his thumb toward Dale. "Watch him."

Nate watched Jesse go, his eyes still burning from the weight of Ryan's stare. It clung to him like smoke, heavy and unrelenting. Jesse grabbed a bottle of water, trudged past the flickering firelight, and disappeared into the tangle of wet brush. Nate saw him vaguely—just a shifting outline in the dark—stooping near the edge of the clearing, rinsing his blood-caked hands with slow, methodical movements. Water splashed onto the leaves below, gleaming silver for a heartbeat before being swallowed by the mud.

The fire flickered. Rain fell harder now, drumming on the tarp above Dale and spitting in the coals. The wind shifted. Nate tilted his head up, his cigarette dimming between his fingers. The world felt still—but not calm. The silence between the drops felt loaded, like something holding its breath.

Ryan exhaled a thick stream of smoke that drifted toward Nate's face. Nate didn't move. Didn't answer. But something inside him coiled tight. A second stream of smoke followed, deliberate. Provocative. And then Ryan chuckled low in his throat, a smug, guttural sound that made Nate's skin crawl.

But when Nate finally turned, he saw more than mockery in Ryan's eyes. Beneath the alcohol and bravado, the twitching glances, the jitter in his legs, the restless motion of his fingers—there it was. Fear. Raw and human. Just enough to make Nate realize: Ryan wasn't as sure as he pretended. Not even close.

Still, it didn't matter.

Another puff of smoke hit him.

"You know what, Ryan," Nate muttered, his voice flat, measured. He took a slow drag of his cigarette, the ember flaring in the dark. "Now's probably not the time. But you and I—we've got things we're gonna settle. One way or another."

Ryan leaned forward, grinning wide like a man welcoming a fight. "You're damn right. Been waitin' for a chance to shut you up." He tipped the bottle back, then let some of it slosh to the ground. The dirt drank it with a quiet hiss.

Then—a rustle.

Nate's head snapped toward the trees. His eyes darted to the brush where Jesse had been. Empty.

"Jess?"

Nothing.

Ryan turned sharply. "Shit... Where the hell is he?"

They both froze. Rain drummed. Somewhere in the woods, leaves rustled—a sound not made by wind.

"Jess!" Nate shouted, stepping forward, panic rising like bile in his throat. The trees around him blurred. The clearing tilted.

Then—

A scream.

Sharp.

Wet.

Human.

It split the forest like a blade.

"Jess!" Nate roared and took off, heart pounding.

Ryan bolted after him, shotgun clenched tight in his fists.

Nate couldn't even hear his own thoughts—just the rush of blood, the churn of his boots in mud, the slap of branches against his face as he pushed forward. Through the underbrush. Through the dark. Through the nightmare.

Rain hammered them from all sides. Trees blurred into one another. The ground pulled at their feet. The clearing, the fire—it vanished behind them, swallowed whole by the forest's maw.

Then—a clearing.

Nate was the first to break through the underbrush, his legs burning, lungs scraping with each breath, but he didn't slow. He pushed forward, mind blank except for one name. One thought. Jess. The branches tore at his jacket, rain needled his face, but he kept running.

And then he saw it.

He stopped.

Stopped like something had seized him by the spine and locked him in place.

Jesse was there.

Or what was left of him.

His body lay draped over the twisted roots of a tree, arms askew like discarded tools, bent at unnatural angles. His shirt was torn open, his chest... torn through. Twice. Two ragged holes, pierced clean by something enormous. The wounds were gaping and obscene, and steam rose from the blood pooling beneath him, as if the forest was trying to swallow the warmth of him before it faded completely.

His eyes were open.

Staring.

Mouth too.

As if the scream had been ripped from his lungs—and the silence that followed still echoed in the trees, suspended in the air like mist that refused to lift.

Rain tapped against his face, each heavy drop striking his open eyes and parted lips. They landed with wet, deliberate smacks, beating a rhythm against him that matched the thudding in Nate's skull—a pulsing drumbeat of horror. Each drop felt louder than the last. Louder than breath. Louder than thought.

It was like the storm was trying to wash Jesse away, but he remained. Frozen. Wide-eyed. Gaping. A memory too fresh to fade.

"Jess...?" Nate's voice came out in a broken whisper, brittle as glass. His legs wouldn't move. He couldn't step closer. It was as though the earth itself had risen up and nailed him in place.

"God... Jesse..." he breathed, and then again, barely audible.

Each word fell from his lips like ash.

Behind him, Ryan skidded to a stop. His boots sloshed in the mud. He raised the rifle, whipping it from side to side, but there was nothing. Only trees. Shadows. Rain.

"Jesus. Jesus Christ," he rasped, barely more than a breath. His voice shook as badly as his hands, cracking under the weight of panic. He gasped—harsh, desperate breaths, like a man drowning on dry land. His eyes, wide and rimmed with white, flicked wildly from shadow to shadow.

"What the hell is this?" he barked, louder now, chest heaving. "Where are you, you son of a bitch? Come on! COME ON!" His voice cracked again, sharp as splintered bone. "You hiding? Is that it? Come out and face me, you coward!"

He turned in a slow, frenzied circle, the barrel of the rifle twitching with every movement, his eyes chasing ghosts that hadn't yet stepped into the firelight.

But Nate wasn't listening.

He couldn't hear. Not really. Not the rain. Not Ryan. Not even the sound of his own breath, which came fast and shallow.

He just stared.

Jesse's body looked as if it had been hurled by some colossal force—shattered by something vast, merciless, and terrifyingly precise.

And Nate couldn't look away.

He didn't check the woods. Didn't reach for a weapon. Didn't brace.

None of it mattered.

It didn't matter if something came charging out of the darkness right now, didn't matter if the forest ripped open to swallow them whole. Jesse was dead.

And something deep inside Nate went very, very quiet.

Behind them, the trees seemed to shift.

The forest exhaled.

A ripple passed through the branches—barely a sound, but enough. Enough to know *something else was there.* Just beyond the veil of rain and bark and shadow.

Watching.

Waiting.

Chapter 6:
Eyes in the Brush

The barricade was crude. A jagged ring of broken branches, stripped pine trunks, and snapped limbs piled high around the edge of the camp like ribs around a rotting heart. It wouldn't stop anything that truly wanted in, and they all knew it. But building it had kept their hands moving, had given their fear something to latch onto. A distraction. An illusion of control. And now, with the last limb wedged and the silence returning, it all looked ridiculous.

Evening fell hard in the Appalachian woods. The trees stood darker, heavier, leaning in with the weight of old secrets. The sky had begun its slow retreat behind the mountains, a thin, bleeding edge of sunlight cutting across the distant ridge. Above, clouds churned—low and blue-black, bruised from the inside out—casting a premature dusk over the forest floor. A strange, early twilight that made shadows stretch and breathe like they were alive.

Nate sat by the fire, unmoving. The cigarette hung forgotten between his fingers, its ember long gone, but a thin thread of smoke still rose from it — faint, stubborn, clinging to the last heat. It curled upward in slow spirals, losing shape in the damp, heavy air before dissolving into the silence of the trees.

The rain was lighter now. No longer a downpour, just the steady rhythm of scattered droplets. Here and there, a drop would find its way down through the branches and plink against the tarp or the coals. But the world was wet. Everything soaked. The soil beneath their boots had gone soft and black, the scent of it thick in the air—earthy, cold, and fungal. Moisture clung to the skin like breath. The kind of damp that crept into bones and thoughts alike.

Around him, the forest breathed—but Nate no longer noticed.

He had sunk beneath it, deeper than exhaustion, deeper than fear. The world above felt muffled, like someone had wrapped his head in wool. Sounds reached him distorted and distant: a branch cracking, Dale's ragged wheeze, Ryan muttering to himself somewhere to the left. Everything sounded like it came from underwater.

Somewhere behind the trees, a crow cried—sharp and sudden.

Then the wind shifted, curling through the brush, setting the branches rustling in uneven pulses. The clouds above stirred, slow and heavy, like great bodies turning in restless sleep. Nate tilted his head upward and watched them, eyes half-lidded. The sky felt too low, too close. The clouds sank until it seemed they would brush the tops of the pines, thick as wet wool.

He brought the cigarette to his lips without thinking. Didn't drag. Just held it there, trembling faintly in the corner of his mouth. He stared at the same patch of earth between his boots until it blurred, until the edges of the world melted into each other and time collapsed.

It felt like being submerged. The forest above was still moving—wind, birds, breath—but none of it touched him. Not really. Not anymore.

He wanted to come up for air. He wanted to break the surface. But something was holding him down.

Darkness pressed in at the corners of his eyes. Not sleep. Not quite. A kind of numb pressure, like the night itself had wrapped around his chest. Inside his head, everything was silent. Utterly still.

No thoughts. Just weight.

Then came the face.

Jessie's face.

It didn't appear with any ceremony or vision. It was just… there. Burned into the darkness. Those empty eyes, locked on nothing. That blood, so bright it stained the memory like acid.

Wherever Nate looked—behind his eyelids, into the trees, down at the dirt—it was there. Watching. Bleeding.

His chest tightened, but he didn't cry. Couldn't. The feelings had drained out somewhere along the way. What remained was static. A flat hum of grief so deep it felt like silence.

The world blurred again. Rain on the fire. Crows calling overhead. A gust of wind that moved the tarp with a sigh.

Nate didn't move. He didn't speak. He just stared ahead, into the place where the forest grew too thick for light to reach.

It was like staring into his own mind—and finding nothing but fog.

It started as a sound half-caught in his throat—a breath that didn't quite make it, a syllable shredded by fear. But it forced Nate's gaze to shift, if only for a moment.

A noise nearby. Subtle. Wet.

Dale stirred—then screamed. Raw, broken, full of something that didn't sound human anymore. His hands clutched his side, fingers digging into soaked bandages, and when he pulled them away, they trembled, slick with fresh blood.

He looked down at his hand.

Shaking. Red. Alive.

A shudder ran through him. His breath came in short, uneven jerks, and then—like trying to escape his own body—he flinched hard, swiping at the air, at himself, as though the blood were something alive. He sobbed, just once, sharp and helpless.

Nate heard it—even through the fog in his skull.

That sound didn't belong to pain alone.

It was the sound of a man about to fall apart. *Completely.*

Dale was curled near the fire's dying glow, swaddled in damp blankets and blood-streaked cloth, his face pale as river stone. His lips trembled before sound returned, and when it did, it came rough and broken, the voice of a man who'd already seen too much.

"We're not getting out of here," he rasped.

Nate didn't answer.

Dale's eyes fluttered wide, wild and glistening with a sick sheen. His chest hitched. "We're gonna die out here. All of us. This is it. This is the end…"

He sobbed once—sharp, ugly, raw.

Nate looked down at the half-burned cigarette between his fingers, about to draw—only for a fat raindrop to slap the ember into silence. A hiss. A curl of smoke—and then nothing.

He snorted, almost a laugh, shoved a hand into his jacket, fumbled for the pack. The motion was mechanical. Desperate in a quiet way. Fingers trembling as he struck the lighter, cupped it against the wind, brought a fresh stick to life. The smoke curled upward, thin and unsteady. He took a long drag, eyes heavy-lidded, watching Dale as if from behind glass. Something in that stare wasn't quite indifference—but it wasn't sympathy either. It was memory. A foggy kind. Something from a world far away.

Across the clearing, Ryan whipped his head around.

"Shut up," he barked.

He stood in the center of the camp now, tense as a live wire, shoulders knotted with silent rage. His rifle shifted constantly in his grip, always adjusting, like even steel couldn't sit still in his hands. He scanned the perimeter, eyes flaring wide one moment, narrowing the next—searching for ghosts among trees.

Then he moved again.

Not walked—ran. Quick steps, fast and sharp. He darted to the edge of the makeshift barricade—nothing but sticks jammed into the mud and hope—and began fiddling with it again. Rearranging, repositioning, gripping each branch like it might save them, pressing them into the earth with care that was almost obsessive. A man reordering deck chairs while the ship already tilted.

Every few seconds, he glanced back toward the woods. Expecting something. Readying himself.

His breathing came in sharp puffs—fast, forceful. Like each breath was expelled just to prove he was still alive.

"You know it too," Dale whispered, trembling. He pushed himself halfway upright, grimacing as blood seeped anew from his bandaged side. His voice cracked under the weight of terror. "We're not getting out... We never should've come. It's watching us. It's playing with us—like it knows... it knows."

He choked back a sob. "God, I don't want to die…"

"Dale—" Nate murmured, barely audible over the hiss of the rain.

"Don't leave me!" Dale shrieked suddenly, his voice slicing the quiet like a knife. "Please, don't leave me here! Don't let it get me—don't let it—"

"Jesus, Dale." Nate's voice snapped louder than he expected, harder than he intended. "No one's leaving you, alright? Just shut up already."

The words struck the clearing like a whipcrack. Sharp. Cold. Echoing in the wet stillness. Even Ryan stopped—froze mid-motion—staring at Nate like he'd just spoken in another language.

Dale recoiled as if slapped. His voice fell to nothing.

The forest listened.

Rain ticked softly on tarps and leaves. Somewhere in the distance, a branch creaked.

Ryan resumed moving, but slower now—more methodical. He paced the camp's edge like a wolf penned in too long, eyes darting between the trees. Water beaded on his shoulders, slicked down his beard, but he didn't flinch. His whole frame vibrated with energy—pent-up, predatory.

Ryan adjusted one of the sticks again—one that had sagged just an inch too far down the barricade. His hands moved with the same twitchy precision, like fixing that one branch might keep the world from caving in.

Nate watched him.

Just barely.

A crooked, skeptical smirk touched the corner of his mouth—gone almost as soon as it appeared. He shifted with a quiet sigh, legs stretched out, the cigarette burning steady between his fingers.

"You think all that stacking's gonna stop it?" he muttered, eyes still on the fire.

"We're decorating a tomb."

Ryan froze.

The muscles in his neck stood out like cords, his jaw locked, his lips tight. He was ready—for what, he didn't know.

Then his eyes locked on Nate.

And they stayed there.

Not just a glance—no. This was something colder. A slow, piercing stare that drilled into Nate's skin like it meant to peel him apart. Like Ryan wasn't just looking at him, but through him—trying to find the part that would crack first.

Nate met his gaze.

Didn't look away.

They stayed like that. Just a beat too long. Long enough to mean something neither of them would say aloud.

Long enough for the woods to breathe again. Long enough for the rain to hush.

Nate's eyes opened a little wider. "What?"

Ryan stepped closer, the muzzle of his rifle rising—not in aim, but in accusation. "You," he snapped. "I'm looking at you, Nate. You completely lost it, huh? What the hell is wrong with you?"

He jabbed the rifle toward the pile of damp branches lashed against the clearing's edge—haphazard defenses built on desperation. "You're just sittin' there with your little cigarette while I'm out here busting my ass putting all this shit together?"

Nate blinked once in reply. His lips pressed tight, a faint crease in his brow. Then he took another slow drag, smoke curling up past his temple. A slight shake of the head followed—tired, dismissive. Like explaining anything at this point would be a waste of air.

"That's not how this works," Ryan growled, stepping closer. "We're drowning out here, and you—you're sittin' there like some smug bastard on dry land, watchin' us sink like it ain't your problem."

He jabbed a finger at Nate's chest, voice rising.

"You think you're better than us? That it's all beneath you? You won't even pick up a damn gun!"

He laughed once—short, cold, sharp.

"You're not calm. You're not wise. You're just scared, Nate. A coward too proud to admit he's useless."

He leaned in, breath hot.

"Hidin' behind cigarettes and that blank stare like that's gonna save you when it comes."

He stepped in.

Closer.

The rifle dipped just a fraction—but enough to matter.

"And if you look at me like that again, I swear to God, I'll stub your little cigarette out in your damn eye. You hear me?"

Nate's gaze lifted again. Calm, but sharper now.

Ryan's face was red—veins taut, jaw flexing, that feral look in his eyes like something was unraveling behind them. He was sweating, but not from heat. It wasn't just fury anymore. It was something looser. More erratic. Like he was holding himself together with spit and grit.

"What do you want from me, Ryan?" Nate asked, his voice flat but pointed. "This?" He gestured to the stacked branches with a twitch of his fingers. "If it wants in, those twigs aren't gonna stop it. You know that."

"Oh, do I?" Ryan stepped in again—half a foot now between them—and shoved the barrel forward until it nudged Nate's chest. "Then maybe you've got all the answers. Maybe you know exactly what to do."

Nate's voice snapped, sharp and cutting, just as Ryan shoved the barrel harder into his chest—slow, deliberate, grinding it in like a challenge.

Without hesitation, Nate slapped the rifle aside with a sudden, explosive motion, his breath flaring from his nostrils.

"Get that damn thing off me!" he barked, the words cracking out like a shot.

Ryan didn't back down. His lip curled into something between a sneer and a snarl.

"Afraid? Good," he hissed. "Tyler said animals can smell fear. So whatever the hell that thing is… it'll come. And I'll be waiting."

He didn't smile. Not really. His mouth twisted, but it was all nerves and teeth.

Then the rifle came back up—slow, steady—rising until the muzzle hovered inches from Nate's face, so close he could see the cold metal blur just beyond his eyes.

"You're bait," he said, almost gently. "You sit here. I wait."

From the side, Dale whimpered.

"Ryan—" Nate's voice shifted, cautious now but laced with steel. "One more time. Get that damn thing off me."

He raised his hand and pointed to the barrel. "I'm not the bait. None of us are spectators. We're all the damn bait. And it's coming. Sooner than you think."

Ryan squinted, eyes twitching back toward the trees. He hesitated—then pulled the rifle aside with a grunt, like the tension had burned out just enough to release his grip.

Nate stubbed out his cigarette on a nearby stone with slow, deliberate pressure. The hiss was sharp. Final.

For just a second, his hand trembled—barely. He steadied it with a quiet breath, almost imperceptible, giving himself the space of a heartbeat to pull back into place.

His eyes flicked toward Ryan again. The weight behind that glance wasn't just irritation—it had teeth. Something sharp itched just behind his expression, but he swallowed it down.

Not now.

Not yet.

"Alright," he muttered. "Let's talk real for a second. What do we know about it? The monster. The thing."

Dale coughed. It wasn't a normal cough—this one came from deep inside, ragged, wet, and wrong. Nate turned. Dale looked smaller now, like some part of him had already started fading. His skin was grayer. Sunken. Drenched in fever and fear.

He looked like something that had been forgotten in the rain.

His mouth moved, lips trembling with words that never made it out.

But Ryan cut across him.

"Nothing," he spat. "Same thing I said before. Not a damn thing."

He checked the rifle, hand twitching at the bolt. "But one thing I do know?"

His voice lowered.

"If it breathes, it can bleed."

He looked up, jaw clenched like a vice.

"And if it bleeds…"

A beat.

"I can shoot it."

He hefted the rifle like punctuation—like every motion needed emphasis now, a final word. *A warning.*

Nate watched him, lips tightening into something close to disbelief. There was less and less of the man left in Ryan with every passing minute. His movements had gone jerky, twitchy. He blinked too fast. Kept shifting his weight from foot to foot like the ground itself made him restless.

He flinched at sounds that weren't there. Sniffed the air like a dog catching scent. His neck craned at strange angles, eyes darting through the trees with quick, stuttering snaps. At one point, he bared his teeth. Not a smile. Something else. Something that didn't belong on a human face.

It was like the forest had crawled inside him.

And now it was wearing his skin.

Nate said nothing for a long time, then finally spoke—his voice quiet, sure.

"I think Tyler was talking about it. About this. The monster."

He swallowed.

"The one who hunts the hunters."

Dale whimpered from his place near the fire. His lips trembled before the words made it out.

"Yeah…" he breathed, as if the memory of it physically hurt. "That's it. It's real. And it's coming back—God help us, it's coming back."

He clutched at his torn belly, and the pain dragged a scream out of him that seemed too raw for a man to make. Nate turned, just for a second, instinct pulling him toward the sound—

That's when he felt it.

A shift.

Not a sound. Not a snap of twigs or rustle of leaves. Just… presence.

The trees ahead didn't look quite the same.

Branches that had been familiar were suddenly foreign. The forest, ever-changing, ever-breathing, seemed to realign itself in front of him—as if it were watching, adjusting, responding. The shapes of trunks and thickets blurred, flickering like shadows behind candlelight.

And then—*movement.*

Just a flicker at the edge of vision.

He turned toward it, even before his brain fully registered what he'd seen. Something primal reacted first.

For a breathless moment, the world went silent. Trees shimmered with dew and darkness.

Then he saw it.

Not clearly. Not fully.

Just a gap between branches.

And in that gap—**eyes**.

Two burning cinders. Low to the ground. Glowing softly, like coals under ash. They didn't blink. Didn't move. Just stared.

Nate felt something seize in his chest.

There was nothing else to see. No sound, no shape. Only those eyes. Hanging in the black like they belonged to the forest itself.

He stepped forward without realizing it, breath shallow, legs moving on instinct. Those eyes held more than malice. More than hunger or rage.

There was memory in them.

Something older.

Something that had been here long before them.

The forest, come alive. The forest, stepping forward.

And then it did.

From the shadows, it emerged—massive, deliberate, and terrifying in its stillness.

The boar.

Not just big. Impossible.

It loomed, massive—easily over eight feet from snout to haunch, its shoulders rising nearly to a man's chest. Its back bristled with coarse, rain-soaked hair, clumped with filth and streaked dark with old blood. Its tusks gleamed in the moonlight, each one as long as a man's arm and curved like ancient blades. The muscles beneath its thick hide moved like plates of armor, rippling with coiled power.

And those eyes—those terrible, burning eyes—never left him.

Its breath came low and slow, but it didn't sound like breath at all.

It sounded like the mountain exhaling.

Like the earth itself shifting beneath their feet.

The dirt seemed to pulse with every inhale.

It was looking at him.

Through him.

Nate couldn't move. Couldn't even blink.

His legs felt nailed to the soil, as if the earth itself had clenched around his feet. His lungs forgot how to draw air. That stare—those ember-lit eyes locked with his—froze time itself.

The forest went still.

Not quiet—*still.*

Every leaf, every drop of rain, every breath of wind held in place.

As if the woods were waiting, too.

Dale saw it too.

He jerked violently, a raw cry escaping him as pain flared through his side. "Oh God," he moaned, clutching at his torn stomach. "It's here. It's here."

His breath broke into panicked, stuttering gasps. Every inhale caught like it might be his last.

Ryan spun, his rifle snapping up with a speed born of pure instinct. "Where?! Damn it, where is it?!"

"There," Nate whispered, barely moving. "Right there."

But by the time Ryan turned his head, it was gone.

Only trees.

Dense brush and timber, too thick, too still. Shadows layered on shadows, the forest holding its breath. Every branch looked hostile, every leaf like it might conceal something more. Even the air felt sharper, heavier.

Dale collapsed backward, his face gone pale as ash. "Oh God... we're dead. That's it. We're all dead."

No one answered.

Above, the sky had begun to rot.

Not from sunset, but from clouds crawling over the peaks like bruises blooming across bone. Thunder grumbled somewhere behind the ridge, deep and disinterested.

The Appalachians loomed, great knuckled hills slouching toward the heavens. Trees clawed upward, ancient and grim, older than names.

The wind had stopped.

No birds. No bugs.

Just the sharp tick of rain.

Just the fire, nervous and spitting in the dusk-thick gloom.

And then... something breathed.

A low, massive exhale.

Not from lungs—from something larger. It rolled across the trees like a tremor, vibrating through bone and bark alike.

The ground trembled.

At first it was barely there, a quiver in the soles of their boots. Then a strange rustling, like wind with weight behind it. And then came the crash.

A sound like the world splitting open.

A pine tree jerked—just slightly at first, like something had brushed it from beneath.

Nate squinted, instinct tensing before thought caught up.

Another twitch.

Then a sharp, wet crack, loud and sudden, like a bone breaking inside the world itself.

The trunk shifted. Groaned.

And then—slowly, with a deep, splintering wail—it began to fall.

Not drop. Not tumble.

Lower.

Like something massive was pushing it, guiding it, forcing it down inch by inch with cruel intent.

Branches screamed as they were ripped free, their green fingers clawing at the air.

Leaves shredded in the rush, spinning like torn paper in a storm.

Twigs snapped in a chorus of brittle fractures, dry and sharp.

Then came the impact.

The trunk slammed into the edge of the camp with the weight of a landslide.

The barricade exploded—sticks and lashings flying apart like toy pieces.

Splinters ripped through the air.

Pine needles and dirt ballooned into the clearing, choking the firelight, burying everything in wet, living debris.

The smell of torn bark—raw and resinous—flooded their lungs.

Nate yanked Dale aside just in time.

The tree slammed down a few feet from where they'd been. The shockwave of it threw up wet earth in clumps, peppering them in mud and pine. Leaves stuck to Nate's neck, and the taste of smoke turned to soil on his tongue.

Ryan had leapt away, rolling and springing back to his feet like a feral thing. He turned, eyes wide, teeth bared, and opened fire.

One shot cracked through the trees.

Then another.

Then another.

"Where the hell is it?!" he screamed, emptying blind fury into the green.

The woods gave no answer.

Nate backed up until his spine hit bark. Cold and wet.

He couldn't move. Couldn't speak.

His lungs fought for air, but his chest felt bound, like the whole forest was leaning against him.

His heartbeat hammered, loud in his skull.

He wiped at his face, trying to brush off dirt and pine needles. "Is everyone alive?" he gasped.

Dale didn't answer, just lay there, heaving. His jaw shook, teeth chattering, eyes wide.

Ryan was still staring into the woods, rifle up, unmoving now. His jaw clenched so tight it made a sound.

Nate slid down the tree, collapsing until he was sitting in the mud, arms wrapped around his knees. Rain hammered his scalp, soaked through his shirt. Around him, chaos.

The fallen pine took up nearly the whole clearing. What was left of their tents had been crushed. Supplies scattered. The barricade—what little defense they had—was now a memory.

The forest had delivered its message.

It could crush them at any moment.

Like insects.

And the strangest thing?

No tracks.

The soil was torn from the impact—but nothing else. No prints. No drag marks. Not even a broken path.

Only the smell.

Rotting blood and wet earth.

The scent clung to them. To their tongues. Their eyes.

The trees looked wrong now. Tilted. Slightly off. Some bent the wrong way, others too still, as if caught mid-motion and frozen. The sound of the wind, when it returned, came warped, bent around corners that hadn't been there before.

Nate blinked hard. Tried to clear it from his mind. Tried to tell himself it was panic. Shock.

But he wasn't sure anymore.

He wasn't sure what was real, and what was just the forest changing around them.

Nate swallowed hard.

Something was coming.

He could feel it.

His thoughts weren't even thoughts anymore—just images, spinning in a tight, spiraling loop. The dead moose. The black-feathered mess of ravens. A wing lay on the blood-soaked earth, fluttering in the wind like a torn flag. Blood. Tyler's ruined body—scattered, shredded. Then Dale. Bleeding into the dirt. Jesse—

Nate flinched. That memory struck deeper.

His eyes stared through the trees, but saw nothing.

Only red. Only loss.

And then the boar. The thing that hunts the hunters. Those eyes—not just wild. Not just savage. Ancient. As if the woods themselves had arrived.

Somewhere behind his forehead, he felt something crack.

Not physically.

Like a window, spider-webbed with pressure.

And then Jesse's voice.

So close.

So real it felt like he was standing behind him, his breath brushing his neck.

"Be different. But don't stand still while this thing eats us alive. Or are you just gonna sit there and watch?"

The words hit like lightning.

Something surged through him—hot, sharp, alive.

Not courage. Not clarity.

Just motion.

A refusal to be swallowed by stillness.

He turned.

The clearing was in ruins.

Their camp was gone.

And somehow, that made it easier.

He looked at Dale.

Broken. Alive.

Still breathing.

Beside him, Ryan twitched like a live wire—tense, fraying, and filled to the brim with barely-contained fear.

Nate looked up.

"We have to move," he said, voice hoarse.

"Now. We carry Dale. We leave. Right now."

Above them, the forest closed in.

And somewhere in the dark,

Chapter 7:

The Long Walk Nowhere

The forest did not let them go. Not that night.

They left behind the ruin of their camp, stepping into a darkness that felt older than time. It wasn't just night—it was something else entirely. The shadows were too thick, the silence too deep. No stars. No moon. The rain had stopped, but the damp still clung to the air like breath against the back of the neck. Wet branches hung low like arms, moss spread thick beneath every footstep, and the trunks of trees glistened with a slick sheen. Clouds rolled above like a second canopy, low and heavy, threatening to collapse with their own weight. Sometimes, the mist would part just enough to reveal a patch of sky darker than anything below. As if even the heavens wanted no part of this.

Nate felt it crawling along his skin—that wrongness. The sense that each breath was borrowed, and each step was being watched. The air was syrupy, too thick, like it had to be swallowed, not inhaled. Every footfall sank deeper into the muck. Every movement felt like dragging his body through molasses.

Ryan led the way. His pace was quick, too quick for caution, almost manic. His boots stumbled often, snagging on roots, slipping on moss. He twitched, flinched, spun to check behind him like a spooked animal, eyes wide, whites flashing even in the dark. His rifle clacked with every adjustment, the barrel swinging wildly left and right as if something might lunge from the trees at any moment.

Nate watched him from a few paces back, unnerved. Ryan's muttering reached them in fits and starts—nothing clear, but enough to chill the air around them further. Dale whimpered under Nate's arm, his weight growing heavier by the minute.

Nate hauled him through the underbrush, one arm wrapped beneath Dale's shoulders, the other cinched around his chest. Every few steps, Dale stumbled, dragging them both down an inch. Nate's legs ached, his knees felt filled with lead. His breath came short, uneven. Sweat trickled from his hairline, mingling with dirt and damp. He wiped his brow with a trembling hand, only to find his fingers slick with more than just sweat.

The forest whispered around them. Not voices, but suggestions. Branches that shifted without wind. Leaves that trembled at nothing. The creak of bark straining under unseen weight. A crack. A breath. Then silence.

Nate's heart began to hammer, not in panic, but in that deeper place beneath fear—the part that knows. That remembers what came before language. The part that understands what it means to be prey.

This wasn't fear. It was worse. It was knowing they were already too deep. That nothing ahead could save them. That whatever watched from the shadows wasn't just waiting—it was guiding.

The sensation built in his gut like a coil tightening. As if something ancient stirred below the forest floor, following each of their footfalls. As if the darkness itself was hungry.

And still, they walked.

Because stopping was death.

And something worse might be catching up.

Dale groaned with every step, each jolt rattling through his ribs like glass in a bag. Sweat clung to his pale skin like morning dew, his hair slicked and plastered to his forehead. His breathing was shallow now, not just from pain, but from something else—something clawing up through him, hollowing him out from the inside. Every few feet, he'd clutch at his stomach and let out a stifled whimper, like the pain itself was burrowing deeper.

Nate didn't know if it was the fever or the fear that was doing more damage. Honestly, he was surprised Dale could still move at all. He looked like a man held together by memory alone. His limbs barely cooperated—half-dragged, half-driven by something that wasn't survival instinct so much as momentum. And still, with Nate propping him up, they staggered on.

The forest was a noose. And the loop was tightening.

Ryan had pushed ahead, not looking back, his silhouette lurching in and out of the shadows. Nate could still see him—barely—but every few steps it felt like the trees might swallow him whole.

His own legs trembled, muscles twitching with fatigue. Each uneven drag of Dale's weight sent a jolt through his spine. He staggered, caught himself, staggered again. Strength bled from him like warmth into the damp night.

His skin crawled. Sweat clung to him despite the cold, and he wiped his brow with a trembling hand. Then tried to breathe deep—only to find the air thick and thin all at once, as if the forest had stolen half of it for itself.

And then—

«Stop.»

Dale jerked out of Nate's grip with sudden force, stumbling sideways. He backed against a thick pine, his breath hitching in shallow, ragged bursts. For a second, Nate just stared. Dale looked like something wilted, some dying thing barely clinging to the shape of a man.

Then Dale slumped to the ground.

«I—I can't,» he whispered, one hand clawing into the earth, the other still pressed to his stomach. «We're not getting out. We're not.»

Nate moved toward him. «Dale, come on, we just have to—»

«No. No!» Dale's voice cracked like ice underfoot. He stared at the trees, wide-eyed. «It's the same. All of it. We passed that stump an hour ago. Or yesterday. I don't— I don't know.»

He shook his head like trying to rattle something loose. Nate crouched beside him, but Dale wouldn't look at him.

«We're meat,» Dale muttered. «Just... walking meat.»

Nate's heart thumped.

«Dale. Look at me. You're not—»

«It already chose us.»

Ryan's voice sliced through the tension like a saw.

«Then lie down and die already!» he snapped. His silhouette loomed out of the dark, rifle raised—not aimed, just trembling with fury. «All this whining and sobbing—shut up! Shut up! It hears you!»

Dale stared past him now, into the trees, his lips moving silently, his body trembling. His face was slick with sweat. His teeth chattered, though the air wasn't cold anymore.

Nate reached for his shoulder. «We're not done. You hear me? You can't quit here. Not now. Not like this.»

But Dale was barely listening. He looked up at Nate, eyes unfocused.

«It's already inside the woods,» he whispered. «It's pulling us in.»

Nate's face twisted—not in anger, not quite—but something close. Like the start of a wince he didn't want anyone to see. A nerve twitched in his cheek. He clenched his jaw and looked away, the words Dale had just muttered too close to what he'd already been thinking.

"Oh, that's just what we needed right now," Nate snapped, voice sharper than he meant—more fear than fury. He turned toward Dale, his expression tightening like a rope. "Dale, please... seriously. It's shitty enough out here without you going full prophet. Just—just keep walking. Alright?"

Dale didn't move.

He sat slumped against the base of a tree, arms folded tight across his chest like he was trying to hold something in—or keep something out. His shoulders trembled, small, uneven jerks that betrayed how close to unraveling he really was.

"No. I know," he wheezed, eyes darting to the trees. "It's in the trees. I feel it, Nate. I feel it everywhere. We're already dead."

Nate saw it now—Dale's whole body was shaking. Barely holding together.

"Dale…" Nate exhaled, voice dropping, weary. "We have to move. That's it. Just move forward, and we'll find a way out. You hear me?"

He reached out his hand.

"Come on. Let's go."

But Dale didn't take it.

He just stared. Frozen.

Footsteps sloshed through the wet ground, and then Ryan's voice came in like a slap.

"So what the hell is going on?" he barked, limping once, then again, before stomping over with heavy steps. He planted himself between them like a stormcloud ready to burst, jaw tight, eyes flaring with that same wired fury that never quite left his face.

"What, you wanna stay here?" He gawked at Dale, then shot a look at Nate. "This for real?"

"Dale, get up," Nate barked, trying to grab him by the arm, but Dale pulled away—flinching like an animal too far gone. "Ryan, help me. He's not right— he's spiraling. Dale, for God's sake—calm down."

But Dale was unraveling.

His skin had flushed a violent shade of red. His eyes watered and rolled, glassy with panic. He wasn't just scared—he was breaking, all at once. Like something inside had finally snapped. His breath came in short, ragged hitches, and his mouth twisted in a silent cry of something that wasn't anger, or grief—but the raw intersection of both.

Ryan's grip tightened around the rifle. His eyes darted from tree to tree. He was breathing hard now, like a man on the edge of snapping.

"It's close," he muttered. "It's in here with us. Watching. Just waiting for one of us to fall."

Then he turned to Dale, voice cracking like a whip.

"If you're not coming, I don't give a shit."

He spat into the mud, lips curled in disgust.

"Drop him here. Let's go."

Nate snapped his head toward him, disbelief flashing in his eyes.

"What did you just say?"

Ryan stared back, unbothered—like he genuinely didn't understand what the problem was.

"You deaf? We need to move, damn it. Can't you see we're knee-deep in this shit? And he's dragging us down."

He held Nate's gaze for a beat longer, then rolled his eyes hard, like the whole thing bored him.

"Oh God. Hell—fine. Rot with him, Nate. Stay here and waste time."

He turned away with a bitter laugh.

"You wanna hold hands in the dark and wait to be gutted, that's on you. I'm moving. Alone's better."

Nate stared at him—stunned for a breath—then something stirred in his chest. A scraping. Familiar. Ugly.

"Are you serious right now?"

Dale whimpered behind him. "It's gonna kill us. It sees us... you feel it? It's out there..."

He lifted a shaking finger toward the dark.

Nate stepped toward Ryan, jaw set.

"You really said that out loud?" he asked, slow and sharp.

"Damn right I did," Ryan growled, rounding on him. His voice hit like gravel thrown in a face. "You pissed, snowflake? You'd rather we all drag around dead weight through cursed woods while he babbles like some Appalachian messiah?"

He jabbed the rifle toward Dale. Not to shoot—just to emphasize.

"Jungle law, baby. Strong survive. Or what—" he laughed, bitter and ugly— "you think if you two cry hard enough, I'll sit here and weep with you?"

His eyes flared—bright, wild, glittering like glass ready to shatter.

Then a jolt ran through him—he twitched, shoulders jerking like he'd been shocked. His boots shifted. His knuckles whitened around the stock of his gun.

"We have to go. I'm going. With or without you."

Nate stared at him hard, the tension in his shoulders coiling tighter with every word.

"Ryan," he said slowly, deliberately, "I really hope there's still a drop of reason left in you. We're not getting out of this alone. None of us will."

Ryan grinned—crooked, sharp, a little too wide.

"Oh, I gave you the choice, didn't I?" He gestured vaguely toward the woods, then looked back at Nate, grin still twitching.

"You're welcome to follow me, suit boy. Unless you think the whole thing collapses if you're not the one calling the shots. That it, Nate?"

His smile faltered for just a heartbeat—just enough to reveal the fracture underneath. And Nate saw it then.

Behind Ryan's eyes, something wasn't tracking. Something wasn't... there.

"I'm just trying to stay sane," Nate said through gritted teeth, his voice a low growl. "That thing—whatever the hell it is—it's not hunting for food. It's not instinct. It's punishment. Retribution."

Ryan barked a laugh, short and brutal.

"Retribution?" he echoed, voice climbing with bitter amusement. "What is this, Sunday school?"

He took a step closer, teeth bared.

"Get your head on straight, Nate," Ryan growled. "This ain't some ghost story. It's a damn hunt. And we're the ones being hunted."

Nate's eyes narrowed. "Tyler warned us."

Ryan scoffed, voice full of acid. "Oh, here we go. Again with that crap." He threw his hands out. "Don't bring Tyler into this, man. He's dead. You know what I say?"

He jabbed a finger toward his rifle, knuckles white.

"It's a boar. Big, small, flying or glowing—I don't give a shit. Any pig that comes near me is gonna meet this."

He slapped the rifle hard.

"That's the difference between you and me. You're scared. Panicking. I don't do fear. I do bullets. So either we move or you stay here and rot. I don't care."

"You know what?" Nate grunted, struggling to lift Dale, who hung limp in his arms—too weak to stand, too heavy to carry. His knees nearly buckled beneath the weight.

"The moment I saw you, I knew what you were. A bastard. Through and through."

He staggered a step, breath catching in his throat, but held Dale upright, if only barely.

"And now? Now I'm just sure of it."

He paused, breath steaming, arms shaking.

"But I'll still say this—" he sucked in air, words rasping through clenched teeth "—Tyler said... those who break the rules... those who mock the forest, who take more than they're owed..."

He looked Ryan dead in the eye, his voice hoarse, thick with strain.

"That thing comes for them. It comes. And it kills."

Ryan let out a sharp exhale. A laugh. A snarl.

"Jesus," he spat. "You know what the real rule is?"

He stepped forward, voice growing—rough, hoarse, more beast than man now.

"Kill, or die. That's it. No spirits. No riddles. Just nature. Cold. Simple."

His eyes landed on Dale like a threat.

He pointed the rifle down—not to shoot, but to show. To say it loud without words.

"Drop the deadweight!" he barked, voice sharp as broken glass. "Or he'll drag you down with him. That's how it works out here. The weak don't make it."

Nate's hands shook as he struggled to keep Dale upright. "Ryan… can we just go, alright? Just—move."

But Dale slipped from his grip—collapsed like something drained dry. He crumpled at Nate's feet with a muffled groan, limp and bloodied. For a second, Nate just stood there, fists clenched, breathing hard.

Ryan gave a low, mocking laugh.

"Told you."

Nate spun around. "Damn it, Ryan—just shut up, will you?" His voice cracked, loud, raw. "I'm trying to keep us alive," he added, lower now. "Not tear each other apart."

Ryan's laugh came fast, barking out like a broken engine.

"Funny. Coming from a guy who won't even lift his damn rifle."

Then he stepped forward—deliberate, slow, like a challenge carved into the mud—and fixed Nate with a stare. Not loud. Not wild. But sharp. Focused. The kind of look that reached past skin and bone and scraped at something buried deep.

And it moved in Nate—stirred something raw, something he'd tried to keep dead and down. But it rose now. Fast. And it hurt.

Nate looked at the ground. Then up. Steady. "You really wanna do this now?"

Ryan stepped in, eyes flaring.

"Been wanting to do this for a while."

He shoved Nate hard—quick, rough, not meant to injure, just to humiliate. But it struck something deeper.

And something snapped.

Nate didn't want this. He knew the second he moved, it would mean giving in—to rage, to exhaustion, to everything they'd buried since the first scream in the trees. But he couldn't stop. Not this time.

Nate staggered a step, caught himself. His breath steamed in the cold.

Then he stepped forward.

"That's it?" he muttered, voice low and hard. "You gonna keep swinging at ghosts… or take a real swing?"

Ryan didn't wait.

His fist shot forward—wild, grazing Nate's shoulder—but Nate was already moving. He barreled into him, both of them crashing sideways into the muck. The ground exploded in a spray of mud. Dale shouted something behind them—frantic and broken.

They grappled in the dark like feral dogs, no rhythm, no form—just teeth bared and knuckles flying. Nate slammed a heavy blow across Ryan's jaw, then another to his ribs. Ryan staggered, lips pulling back in a hiss—but then he surged forward like a beast unchained.

He tackled Nate with his full weight, driving him down, pinning him with brute strength.

Then came the fist.

And another.

A third, heavier—crushing. Nate's ears rang, stars burst across his vision. His head cracked against the earth, and cold mud swallowed his cheek. Blood filled his mouth. He couldn't move—barely even think. Ryan sat on top of him, fists raining down in rage. Nate tried to block—arms flailing, instinctive—but everything blurred, spinning in red and black.

Then—

A sound.

Not loud. Not sharp.

Just... something.

Faint. Wrong. From the woods.

Ryan froze, mid-swing. Still straddling Nate. His chest heaved. He turned his head—slow, confused.

Nate blinked against blood and blur and followed his gaze.

Shapes. There were shapes.

Out there, in the dark.

Something shifted—shadow inside shadow. Moving.

Nate's brow was split open. His nose felt shattered, blood dripping down his chin. Every breath rattled.

And then—the night changed.

It didn't creep.

It struck.

First, a tremor. Faint. A vibration underfoot like the first murmur of a distant avalanche. Then stronger—rhythmic, massive. The ground seemed to breathe. Trees groaned. Branches flexed as if bracing for something.

And then came the roar.

Not a sound—a presence. A violent, thundering shock that rolled through the forest and shook Nate to his core.

Nate saw Dale collapse against the trunk of a tree, clutching his ribs, eyes wide and hollow.

Nate twisted, trying to push Ryan off him, his limbs heavy, breath ragged— still trapped beneath that weight—until the forest exploded.

The Boar tore from the underbrush like a battering ram of tusks and fury, a living nightmare. Fast—too fast. It didn't charge, it detonated, a black blur stitched from shadow and muscle, crashing through the trees as if they were paper.

A grunt. A blur. A roar.

Nate caught it in flashes—burned images behind his eyes.

A ripple of dark muscle.

The glint of blood-slick tusks.

A scream.

Then Ryan was ripped from above him—lifted clean off. His body soared, hit the brush like a sack of shattered bone. A wet crack. Silence. Then groaning.

Nate fell backward into the dirt, heart hammering like a drum.

His hands moved on their own.

The rifle was suddenly there—cold and familiar—gripped tight between trembling palms. He didn't remember picking it up.

His finger found the trigger. His breath caught in his throat.

Eyes blurred from sweat and blood, he squinted down the barrel.

Searched the dark.

Tried to find it again.

His hands were shaking. But they held.

The Boar turned.

It saw him.

And Nate saw it.

Just a shape at first—massive, hulking, wrong. The kind of wrong that didn't scream, but whispered beneath the skin. The forest barely held it. Its form swallowed the dark, branches bowing away like they feared to touch it.

Then—the eyes.

They glowed. Not like fire. Not like an animal.

They burned low and steady, two coals in the black, watching.

Not wild.

Not furious.

Something deeper. Older. A gaze that didn't just see Nate—it measured him. Judged him. Like the forest itself had opened its eyes and decided to speak.

Nate's breath caught in his throat, frozen.

He tightened his grip on the rifle, finger brushing the trigger, ready—

But he couldn't pull it.

Something deeper than fear held him. Something cold and ancient curling through his chest, whispering: Don't.

A tremble surged through his limbs, like a static charge rolling beneath his skin. His legs shifted—he stepped back, involuntarily. Just one step. But it felt like yielding.

His breathing went shallow. Erratic. His chest rose and fell like he'd just outrun death.

And then—

The thing moved.

A flicker. A blur.

Gone.

The creature vanished, not crashing but gliding—back into the dark it came from, like it had never been.

The silence that followed wasn't calm.

It was listening.

Nate stood motionless, heart hammering.

Then the rifle slipped from his hands, hitting the ground with a soft, final thud.

He stumbled forward, toward the broken form on the forest floor—Ryan, groaning, curled over himself.

Blood dripped from his arm, thick and black in the moonless light. Flesh torn open, bone maybe cracked. But he was breathing. Alive. Somehow.

Ryan didn't speak. Didn't curse. He just sat there for a long moment, hunched, one hand shaking against the mud. His face—usually locked in a snarl—was still.

Not calm.

Just... empty.

And for the first time, Nate saw it.

Not fury. Not defiance.

Just a man who'd believed he couldn't be touched—

—and had been proven wrong.

He pushed up to his knees, swaying, spit and dirt stuck to his face. One eye swollen. But standing.

Nate didn't speak. Didn't move to help.

His gaze was still lost in the trees.

Just wind.

Just branches.

But he knew.

It would be back.

It had seen him.

And it would come again.

Chapter 8:

The Forest Wants Blood

The night stretched on, long past any sense of time. It bled into itself like a wound that refused to clot, thick with silence, thick with breath. The forest no longer whispered. It waited.

Nate sat hunched near the smoldering remains of the fire, arms clutched tight around himself, as if he could keep the cold out by sheer will. His shoulders shook—not just from the chill, but from something deeper, something rooted in the marrow. The air pressed in heavy, a slow, coiling weight that slid through the mist, curling around his ribs, into his blood, into his thoughts. It was everywhere.

He flexed his fingers, slowly, one by one, as if to remind himself they were still there. That he was still here. The cigarette trembled between them, nearly spent. He dragged from it hard, the ember flaring in the dark. The smoke seared his lungs, gave him something solid to focus on. But it didn't help. Not really.

Because every time he closed his eyes, even for a blink, he saw it.

The Boar.

Its shape—a ripple of shadows stitched with muscle. Those eyes, burning like coals, not wild, not furious... just aware. Watching. Thinking.

The trees had cracked once in the dark. Pine splintering like bone.

Now it repeated on loop behind Nate's eyes. The blood. The shattered deer from earlier, torn apart and left as warning. And the raven wing sticking up from the grass—jagged and torn, its feathers limp and wet, swaying in the breeze like it had grown there. Dripping onto red-soaked blades. The stench.

He took another drag. The cherry at the end of the cigarette pulsed like a heartbeat.

It was all connected. Somehow.

They were all links. The moose, the tree, the birds. The boar. Even the silence. Each one a link in some vast, unknowable chain—tightening around them inch by inch. He didn't know what it meant, couldn't trace the pattern, but he felt it tightening all the same. Like something ancient pulling threads.

And they were caught in it. Helpless. Entangled.

Tyler's voice—clearer than it had any right to be—rattled through Nate's skull, syncing with the throb of his pulse. Like it wasn't memory at all, but something happening now, whispering behind his eyes.

Not a bear.

Not a wolf.

...Not a man.

The Blood Tusker.

The Boar That Hunts Back.

A spirit.

A punishment.

A reckoning... in flesh.

Not a bear.

Not a wolf.

Blood Tusker.

Hunts back.

Back...

The words bounced around inside him, folding into each breath, into each tremble of his fingers. Like they'd always been there—just waiting to be remembered.

Then another voice, older. Deeper. Rougher. His father's:

«Courage isn't being unafraid. It's knowing the thing's gonna kill you... and standing there anyway.»

The words struck him like a slap. He grimaced, chest tightening. Something in his heart twisted, painful and raw. Not guilt. Not grief.

Recognition.

«Shit,» Nate muttered, voice hoarse, barely a whisper. He turned his head slowly, eyes flicking sideways.

Dale lay slumped nearby, breath shallow, bandages soaked dark and spreading. His skin had turned the color of ash—waxy, thin, touched by something already too far from life. Every few minutes, his lips moved, whispering sounds without shape, like dream-shreds slipping between worlds. Maybe he was dreaming. Maybe he was already gone.

Nate leaned closer when Dale stirred again. Just a flicker—a twitch of lips, a soft opening of his lids. His eyes stared somewhere past the trees, past the night, unfocused. His mouth moved, breathless, shaping something Nate couldn't hear. Then silence. Eyes closed again.

Ryan was pacing.

Not walking. *Pacing.*

Back and forth in a tight loop, a trench worn through pine needles and damp earth, like fury carving its own orbit. His boots crunched in a rhythm too sharp, too deliberate. As he passed, Nate felt his eyes rake across him—hot, sharp, and empty. A look that didn't carry threat, but something worse: promise.

A cigarette dangled from Ryan's mouth, ash curling downward in a precarious thread. One hand clutched his flask like a sacrament, the other toyed with the chamber of his rifle—click, slide, click—fingers moving with restless precision.

He didn't seem to notice the blood anymore.

It still seeped, dark and slow, from the edge of the bandage wrapped tight around his arm. The cloth had long since turned a rusted shade of red, stiff with dried layers. But if there was pain, he didn't show it. Didn't flinch. Didn't favor the limb.

He moved with too much energy—jittery, wired—his steps too quick, his shoulders twitching. At times he bounced slightly with each step, like something inside him was trying to escape. From pain. From fear. From silence.

From himself.

Metal clicked, slid, clicked again. Over and over. A soft, surgical sound—too precise to be random. It echoed off trees, timed like a metronome for madness. Every few seconds. Then again. And again. He even snorted softly with each cycle, like he was mocking himself—or daring the night to interrupt.

The clicking drilled its way into Nate's skull. A steady, gnawing pulse that began to drown out thought itself. It filled the air, silencing everything else. Dale's breath. The forest. Even the pounding in Nate's own chest began to fall into rhythm with it. Like the world was ticking down toward something.

And still it clicked.

When Ryan stalked past him again, that noise snapping behind him like a tail, Nate finally raised his head. His voice cracked like dry bark.

"Would you stop with the damn clicking?"

Ryan turned, sharp as a blade. His eyes caught the firelight and held it, gleaming with something that went deeper than anger—colder. For a few seconds, he just stared at Nate, blinking slowly, like it took time to pull himself back into the real world. Then he let out a breath, not a sigh but a snort—like a bull before the charge—and stepped forward.

«Oh, is that it?» he sneered. «My rifle bothers you? I bother you?»

Nate held his gaze, jaw clenched. «What the hell does that mean? You finally cracked?»

Ryan stepped in closer, voice tightening like a wire. «No, Nate. You and me— we've got something else going on.»

Nate raised his eyebrows, deadpan, not moving. «Right. You're just insane.

Now do us all a favor and go be crazy over there.» He jabbed a finger toward the tree line. «Hell, head into the woods. That was your big idea anyway, right? Turns out I think it was a damn good one. Walk your crazy ass into that forest and don't come back. We'll all sleep better.»

«Oh no, Nate.» Ryan took another step, their boots nearly touching now. His breath stank of copper and whiskey. «I'm not going anywhere without you.»

«The hell does that mean?»

«It means I finally figured something out. Something I should've seen from the start.»

Nate scoffed, dragging smoke from the corner of his mouth.

«Great. You think I'm gonna ask what that means?»

He shook his head, lips curling.

«Don't flatter yourself. I don't give a damn, Ryan—about your thoughts, your theories, or anything else rotting in that head of yours. Just back the hell off.»

«You didn't shoot,» Ryan said.

Nate blinked. «What?»

Ryan raised the flask and pointed it at him like a weapon. «That thing could've ripped me in half. And you just stood there. And watched.»

Nate wiped his busted nose, the blood tacky on his fingers. For a moment, the image flared again—those eyes, glowing in the dark. He dragged the smoke deeper, trying to bury it. «Go to hell, Ryan. If you hadn't lost your damn mind hours ago, we wouldn't be stuck here. We could've moved. Quietly. Together. But no—»

He gestured to the trees, his voice rising. «—you had to yell, scream, swing your damn rifle like a maniac. Like you wanted it to find us.»

Ryan took another swig. He grinned, but there was no humor in it—just teeth. Something raw flickered in his gaze.

«We were right there,» he said, the words dragging like rusted chain. «On the ground. You and me. Close enough to bleed on each other.»

His eyes narrowed, voice dipping into something low and bitter.

«But it didn't come for you, did it? It came for me.»

Nate's spine stiffened. The look in Ryan's eyes wasn't anger anymore—it was suspicion. Paranoia, blooming like rot.

«What the hell are you talking about?»

Ryan leaned in closer, and Nate could smell the mix of alcohol and dried blood.

"And then," Ryan whispered, leaning in close,

"you didn't shoot."

His breath was sharp with whiskey, voice ragged like torn fabric.

"Maybe you wanted it to get me. Maybe you're letting this thing do your work for you. Let it clean up what you can't."

A pause.

"Everyone's dying around you, Nate. Jesse. Tyler."

He tilted his head, eyes gleaming with something unhinged.

"Who's next?"

He didn't say the last word. He growled it. And his eyes—wide, gleaming, wet with something unspoken—locked on Nate like a trigger pulled half-way down.

Nate's fingers twitched toward his rifle.

Then stopped.

The fire crackled between them.

«You're a sick bastard, Ryan,» he muttered, voice like gravel. Then he flicked his cigarette into the dark and rose to his feet, slow and deliberate.

Ryan's rifle clacked again.

Silence.

Then another click.

Then two.

Ryan squinted into the dark, lips tight, something bitter flickering behind his eyes. Nate noticed the way his whole body drew taut, strung tight as wire.

He stared into the black, his silhouette bobbing and twitching in place, jaw clenched hard, restlessness coiled in his shoulders, in the twitch of his jaw.

Mutterings drifted out—barely words. Just breath shaped by thought and firelight.

The flask knocked gently at his hip, swinging loose, metallic and dull—nearly empty now. He didn't drink from it anymore. Just carried it like a charm, like a weapon, like it had something in it that could keep the dark at bay.

And the fire crackled quietly behind them, the only heartbeat anyone trusted.

The flames shrank for no reason. The firepit was stacked high with fresh wood, yet the glow coughed low and sickly, spitting shadows into the trees like warnings. Nate felt it in his skin—tight, crawling—something was wrong. The night had coiled in on itself, and it was squeezing.

He was ready to meet Ryan again. Fists clenched. Part of him wanted it— wanted to smash that smug, venomous face. There was something growing inside him, dark and sharp-edged. Mean. It scared him. It felt too much like what he saw in Ryan's eyes.

Nate's lips twitched, as if a word tried to escape but couldn't. Ryan saw it. Seemed to read it, too—because he stepped closer, just a hair's breadth, like accepting a challenge. The space between them crackled.

Tension climbed past reason.

And all around, the trees moved.

His knuckles cracked. He was going to do it.

And then—

Dale whimpered. His body convulsed slightly, lips twitching around broken syllables. Nate knelt, trying to make out Dale's pale, blood-drained face in the flickering dark.

«Dale? You okay?»

No answer. Just a soft sound, like breath caught on barbed wire.

"Stop…" Dale whispered. "Stop it... please."

The voice wasn't loud, but it cut through the clearing like a blade. The wind shifted. Branches rustled in response, too slow, too synchronized.

Nate bent close to Dale again. His skin was wet with sweat, mouth open, blinking slowly, like he was halfway somewhere else.

«What is it? What did you say?»

Dale's eyes fluttered. Then the whisper came.

«It's here.»

Nate's breath hitched. «What is?»

«It's here... It's here... It's... here.»

The words rolled through Nate's skull like a mantra etched into bone.

Ryan turned, his face unreadable, lit only by fire and madness. He scanned the tree line, rifle raised, but his hands trembled, and his eyes wouldn't stay still.

Nate saw it—the fear beneath all the noise. Ryan's bravado was cracking.

He stood, slow. His chest ached. Something had shifted.

The air was wrong again.

Not just cold—pressurized.

Like the forest was holding its breath.

The shadows moved differently now. They curved. Bent. Swam. Nate's eyes flicked from trunk to trunk. His heartbeat thudded in his throat.

And across the clearing, the fire cracked sharply.

Its light leapt up—twisting shadows.

And behind them—movement.

A shimmer. A ripple.

Massive.

Alive.

Ryan froze.

So did Nate.

It stood just beyond the tree line.

At first, just a shape—too still to be wind, too large to be anything else. Then it stepped forward.

Black. Massive.

The Boar.

Its bulk shimmered in the uneven firelight. Coarse, matted hide slick with something that glistened like oil. Each breath rolled through its chest in slow waves, muscles flexing beneath skin that looked almost armored. The tusks, long and curved, caught the orange glow like polished bone—wet at the tips.

But it wasn't the size that stole Nate's breath.

It was the eyes.

He knew them. The same eyes that stared at him from the dark that night. The same that pinned him in place, rooted him to the earth. They weren't angry. They weren't hungry.

They were *aware.*

Like the forest had opened its eyes. And decided it was done watching.

Everything had gone quiet again.

Too quiet.

Nate didn't notice at first—too deep in the space behind his own eyes, where the images still burned: the beast, the eyes, the moment he almost pulled the trigger. His breath came shallow, heart still pounding like a warning drum with no message.

Nate's hand shot toward the rifle.

He grabbed it hard, fingers wrapping too tight around the stock. He brought it up slowly, deliberately. The barrel rose like a compass needle, drawn straight to the beast's center.

The grass whispered. Leaves turned overhead. The trees murmured their secrets in the hush. Shadows shifted. The fire hissed low.

The Boar moved.

It stepped forward. Slow. Deliberate. No rush. Its body parting the brush with the ease of something ancient. Regal. Deadly. Each step dragged leaves and branches in its wake. It didn't charge. It didn't snarl. It just walked.

Closer.

Closer still.

Its eyes never left Nate's.

And Nate couldn't look away. He felt his breath catch, his chest lock up. Something older than fear curled around his heart, pulled it down into cold stone.

His shoulders shook. He took one step back.

Then another.

His finger on the trigger faltered. He couldn't feel it anymore. The metal slipped in his grip. He tried to breathe. Failed.

Another step back.

The Boar was close now. Too close. He could see the bristles on its neck. The slick sheen on its tusks. The black in its fur shimmered like ink.

He sucked in air through his teeth, ragged and shallow. Pressed his finger down on the trigger.

Just a little.

Didn't fire.

Couldn't.

His hands wouldn't listen.

He backed up again.

«Jesus Christ,» he whispered.

Then—the thing turned.

No warning. Just a flicker. A blur of shadow and muscle.

Gone.

The trees swayed, leaves rustled, but the Boar vanished into the night like smoke pulled back into the earth. Darkness swallowed the space it had filled. Nothing but the forest now. The same as it was before.

Except it wasn't.

Nate stumbled. Dropped the rifle. It hit the ground with a muffled thud.

He staggered forward, chest rising and falling like he'd been holding his breath too long. Ryan stared at him, eyes wide, jaw slack. Neither of them said a word.

Silence crushed them.

No wind. No birds. No insects. Just the fire popping behind them like a wound trying to close.

And they stood in that stillness, like they'd been trapped in this moment forever.

Dale stirred.

A whisper. "You see it too?"

Nate barely nodded.

"It could've killed me," he murmured.

"But it didn't," Dale rasped. His face twisted with pain.

"Why?"

Nate stared into the dark, eyes wide, unblinking.

"I don't know," he said. "Maybe... maybe it wants me to understand something."

His heart hadn't slowed. It pounded with the same frantic rhythm, like it wanted out of his chest—like it had seen something it was never meant to see, and now it just wanted to run. Escape. Forget.

Ryan cackled. Low and bitter. A sound with no joy in it, only sharp edges and rust.

"Jesus," he muttered, swaying a little as the flask kissed his lips. "Maybe you're more like it than you think. Creeping in the dark. Watching from the damn shadows. Letting everyone else scream while you just stand there—quiet. Clean. Like it's all beneath you."

He stopped. His gaze locked on Nate—suddenly clear. Something passed through his expression. Recognition, maybe. Regret. For half a heartbeat, Ryan almost looked human again.

And then he blinked, and it was gone. Twisted.

The smirk returned—uglier this time.

"But that's it, isn't it?" he hissed. "That's what you are. Just a mask. A husk. Something walking around in Nate's skin. That's why it won't touch you. Hell, maybe it sees one of its own."

Nate swallowed hard, throat dry. His hand clenched into a fist. The other dragged across his face, slow and uncertain, like he was trying to feel if he was still there—still real, still alive. For a moment, the trees held their breath, the shadows stilled. The only sound was the crack of Ryan's uneven breathing and the faint hiss of pine sap weeping in the heat.

Nate didn't speak. He couldn't. His mind hadn't yet caught up to what his eyes had seen. He stared, blinking slowly, like the world might shift back into place if he just held still long enough.

The clearing was quiet again. Not safe—but paused, suspended. As if the forest itself was considering him.

He inhaled—deep, shallow, ragged—trying to steady himself in a reality where a thing of tusks and shadow had just stepped out of the trees and looked into him. And then vanished. Like smoke. Like a dream too heavy to remember.

But something changed *again*.

The wind shifted.

And the silence that followed didn't bring relief. It brought a pause—that coiling breath before the scream.

The trees rustled. Not from wind.

Something moved.

Nate turned, barely fast enough to catch it.

A blur.

A scream.

Dale's body lifted off the earth like it had been yanked by invisible jaws. One moment he was there, limp and whispering.

The next—*gone.*

A wet, tearing sound ripped the night apart. Blood sprayed in an arc across the clearing, painting tree trunks, soaking dirt, raining over leaves like some grotesque baptism. The stench hit a beat later. Familiar. Metallic and thick.

Then came the sound.

Not a roar.

A crunch.

Meat and bone and tendon.

"DALE!"

Nate screamed, legs moving without thought.

Ryan opened fire, bullets cracking the dark like lightning. But there was no form to shoot at. No figure. Just the trees, the black, the afterimage of death.

Nate saw limbs. Shreds of what had been a body.

Then **nothing.**

Only *silence again.*

Only the sucking sound of blood dripping from branches.

Only Dale's name echoing in a throat gone hoarse.

He stared at the ground where Dale had been. A massive pool of blood gleamed in the firelight, soaking into pine needles, staining bark, dripping from grass in thick, syrupy strands. Like the forest had bled with him.

Ryan slowly lowered the rifle. Breath ragged. Eyes wide.

The fire cracked behind them. Too loud. Too small. The trees swayed as if exhaling.

And somewhere deeper in that endless black timber—something watched.

Still hungry.

Chapter 9 :

Red Hunger

The morning was quiet in a way that made Nate uneasy.

Not the haunted silence of the night before. Not the creeping hush that slithered through the trees like fog in a crypt, wrapping around the ribs and whispering things that never quite reached the ears. No—this was different.

This was birdsong. Distant and soft, uncertain, like the forest was testing the idea of peace and hadn't decided whether it would keep it.

Sunlight filtered in through the pines in thin, pale gold shafts, catching on dew-slick leaves and shimmering across the undergrowth like it had something to celebrate. A woodpecker tapped lazily on bark somewhere far off, as though the world hadn't ended a dozen times already in the last three days.

It could've been a good day.

It could've been any day.

And maybe that was the worst part of all.

Nate moved through the woods in slow, steady strides. His boots sank silently into damp moss, the soles swallowing mud without a sound. His shoulders were rigid, the borrowed rifle slung tight across his chest, forgotten weight pressing against forgotten pain. But he didn't feel tired. Not anymore.

He didn't feel his legs at all.

It struck him, strangely, how far beyond exhaustion he had passed. The ache was gone. The burn, the stiffness, even the trembling. Just... gone. And yet, his body moved—forward, always forward—like something deeper had taken over. Some ancient mechanism grinding on autopilot long after the soul had shut down.

The world around him had blurred into a smear of green and gray—branches, mist, endless leaves. The forest no longer seemed made of trees, but of movement. A slow breathing thing with no edge, no center. Just more forest, and more, and more. His thoughts spun like smoke in that fog—barely shaped, too slippery to hold.

But one thought remained. One image, anchored like a hook in the meat of his mind:

The Boar.

He'd seen it.

Not a flash. Not a shadow.

They had looked at each other.

Eye to eye.

It could've killed him. It should have.

But it didn't.

That monster—the thing that tore Tyler in half like wet cloth, that shattered Dale, that dragged Jesse into the brush like a broken doll—*it had seen Nate.*

And walked away.

The name—*Jesse*—landed in his mind like a hammer to the chest.

Nate flinched.

Even now, he couldn't think it fully. Couldn't form the thought completely, couldn't breathe around it. But the truth rose anyway—fast, brutal, sharp-edged like broken bone.

Jesse was *gone.*

The realization didn't just sit on his shoulders. It crushed him. Like a fallen tree. Like the sky itself had dropped. He staggered once, chest tightening, mouth dry, jaw clenched so hard it popped. His vision blurred—not from tears, but from sheer internal collapse. The kind of pain that didn't cry, but simply folded in on itself.

And yet, even through that—one question screamed louder than grief:

Why didn't it kill me?

It could have. It stood right there.

It let me live.

Why?

The question spiraled in his head, tight and fast, like a whirlpool pulling him under. He couldn't escape it, couldn't rise for air. It filled his ears. His chest. His throat. The not-knowing, the not-understanding—it was worse than fear. Worse than guilt. It was incomprehension that flayed him raw.

What did it want?

What did it see in him?

Nate dragged his hands up into his hair, fingers gripping at the roots like he could pull the answer straight from his skull. He closed his eyes, shook his head once—hard. As if he could rattle free the fog. As if clarity waited just beneath the static.

But there was no clarity. Only leaves. Mist. And that thing inside him, spinning.

Behind him, Ryan dragged his feet like something broken.

Each step landed too hard, heavy enough to bruise the silence. His breath came in uneven gusts, a stuttering rhythm like his body couldn't quite keep pace with the frantic churn of his mind. It was the sound of a man unraveling—slowly, stubbornly, violently.

Nate didn't turn. He didn't need to. He heard everything. The shuffle of boots in soft earth. The wet inhalations. And, worse than either—the click.

That same methodical *click* of the rifle's chamber.

Metal sliding against metal in perfect, maddening intervals.

Click.

Pause.

Click.

Pause.

Like a heartbeat for the insane. Or a clock counting down to something Nate didn't want to name.

Ryan muttered constantly now. Low grumbles. Half-laughed curses. Words that slipped from his lips like grease, always there, never clear. Sometimes nearer, sometimes farther, depending on how close he loomed behind Nate's spine. Sometimes just a sniff, a snort. A fume of hot breath too close to ignore.

Nate's jaw clenched.

He said nothing.

But his hands tightened at his sides, fingers brushing bark, twitching like they were testing the weight of fear. A new kind of fear—not the ancient one that crept from the trees, but the kind that came with human eyes. Unpredictable. Feral. And carrying a loaded weapon.

He didn't know when it had started, but Ryan had become just as dangerous as whatever watched them from the woods.

And when the clicks came too close, Nate turned his head. Always just enough to catch a glimpse. Just enough to make sure the madness wasn't yet aimed at his back.

He expected trees, mist, shadow.

But instead, he saw the curve of a familiar branch. A patch of lichen-slick stone. The sharp twist of that same broken pine, still bowed like a snapped knee frozen mid-fall.

His eyes traced the scene, slow and uncertain.

The path was familiar.

Too familiar.

He'd been here before.

Not in a general, this-whole-damn-forest-looks-the-same way, but with certainty that wrapped cold fingers around his throat. These trees. That ridge. That broken trunk.

They had walked this trail already.

A flicker sparked in his mind—quick, jagged, like a dream he hadn't meant to wake from. Jesse laughing. Tyler dragging his boots. Dale humming something tuneless and loud. Shapes in the mist that used to be people. He could see them, still walking ahead of him, still alive in some echo.

His heart kicked harder against his ribs.

Ghosts. Everywhere.

Nate's eyes scanned past each landmark, but only briefly—deliberately. There was no room left for mourning. No space to let memory seep in. If he started pulling at those threads, the whole damn thing would unravel.

And he wanted to live.

He didn't say it.

Didn't think it like a prayer.

But his chest expanded slightly as he drew a deeper breath.

He nodded—almost imperceptibly.

Then kept walking.

Behind him, the muttering grew louder again. Broken syllables tumbling from Ryan's mouth, slurred by exhaustion, bent by something darker. The kind of voice that came from someone teetering too close to the edge.

"Hey," came the voice suddenly, sharper this time. "What the hell are you mumbling?"

Nate blinked.

He hadn't realized he'd been speaking.

He turned, confused. "What?"

Ryan stepped closer, rifle low but not relaxed. His mouth twitched with something between a sneer and a threat. His eyes were bloodshot and wild.

"I said—who the hell are you talking to?"

Nate narrowed his eyes.

"Not you," he muttered, lips twisting in something too tired to be sarcasm.

He turned to keep moving.

And froze.

Mid-step. Mid-breath.

The brush thickened ahead—lush, tangled, alive with the scent of damp pine and earth. A few old-growth trees stood guard, their trunks thick with age, bark dark and craggy like hardened scars. One pine arched low, its massive branch hanging sideways, draped in moss like a withered arm. And just beyond it—through a curtain of dangling needles and drifting green mist—the woods opened.

A clearing.

Wide.

Sunlit.

Still.

And there, resting in the middle of flattened grass, lay a shape both surreal and achingly familiar.

The SUV.

It sat tilted slightly to one side, front tires half-swallowed by mud, streaked in places with old rain and pine needles—but intact. Whole. The windshield caught the light, throwing pale reflections across the clearing like fractured glass. There was no blood. No broken windows.

Just... the vehicle.

Their vehicle.

For one breathless moment, Nate stopped breathing entirely.

His heart slammed hard against his ribs.

His legs felt like they might give out. Not from fear. From something stranger—shock. As if the universe had bent back on itself and offered him an impossible exit.

His eyes locked on the SUV, unable to look away.

It didn't feel like salvation.

Not really.

It felt like the ghost of hope—a delicate thread dropped into an ocean of horror. Thin enough to snap at the slightest pull. Fragile enough to vanish with a blink.

Behind him, Ryan had stopped walking too.

But where Nate stood stunned, Ryan squinted at the vehicle with something colder in his face. A hunter's scrutiny. His hand drifted to his chest, patting down his jacket like searching for reassurance—or distraction. A moment later, a cigarette found his lips, and fire kissed the end of it with a sharp crackle. He inhaled deep. Exhaled smoke through flared nostrils.

Then his gaze slid slowly—deliberately—to Nate.

He didn't speak. Not yet.

But something rooted itself in his posture. In his silence. In his stare.

Nate swallowed hard.

His throat felt like sand.

For a heartbeat, neither of them moved.

Then Nate stepped forward. Slowly. Like crossing a frozen lake.

His eyes never left the SUV.

Each stride was heavier than the last, as if the air itself had thickened. The trees began to pull away on either side, bending back like curtains, as golden shafts of sunlight slipped through the canopy in fractured beams. The clearing stretched out before him—lush, green, impossibly alive.

But the tension in his chest wouldn't ease.

This didn't feel like victory.

It felt like a door cracking open—just wide enough to suggest that behind it waited something worse than darkness.

Still, he walked.

Behind him, footsteps followed.

Heavy. Intentional.

The same *click* of the rifle's chamber. The same breath—fast, feral. Cigarette smoke drifted over Nate's shoulder like a whisper, close enough to feel. Each sound from Ryan was another reminder: the danger wasn't just behind them anymore.

It was right there.

On his heels.

Step by step, they crossed the clearing.

The SUV gleamed faintly in the light, half-sunken but waiting. A monument to everything they'd survived. Or thought they had.

And then—

Nate stepped forward, closer. The sun on his face. Grass bending beneath his boots. His pace quickened, instinct rising up through the numb.

But he didn't make it far.

Because suddenly, something cold pressed hard between his shoulder blades.

Still. Precise.

Metal.

He didn't have to look to know what it was.

The click had stopped.

"Stop right there, hero."

The voice cracked out sharp, too close. Cigarette smoke drifted in with it—thick and bitter, curling around the back of Nate's neck like a warning.

Nate turned. Slowly.

Hands half-raised.

Eyes locked forward.

The muzzle of the rifle was inches from his face now.

"Not so fast," Ryan said, voice low and taut.

His eyes were too wide—white-rimmed, fever-bright. His jaw twitched, like he was chewing something spoiled. The flask on his belt swung, untouched for hours.

His hands trembled—but the rifle stayed steady.

And his face…

The way he looked at Nate hollowed the air between them.

It wasn't rage. Or grief. Not even madness in the usual sense.

It was pleasure.

Not glee. Not a grin. Just a cold, brittle satisfaction—like a starving wolf savoring its prey before the first bite.

He looked at Nate the way a man might look at a deer caught in a snare—already his. Already done.

And the worst part?

He was savoring it.

That stillness—the sharp, fixed stillness of someone who had waited too long for this moment.

The final breath before the kill. Something dark. Hungry. The look of a predator who'd finally cornered his favorite prey.

"Ryan," Nate said evenly, "we can get in that car. Right now. We can leave. Just put that thing down and—"

"Shut up."

Ryan's voice cracked like ice.

"You're not walking out of here. Not this time."

Nate's heart was thudding now, deep and hard. But his voice stayed calm, steady.

"What the hell are you doing?"

For a breath—just a breath—Ryan looked unsteady. His mouth twitched. His lip trembled. For a second, he looked young. Lost. Like a kid who'd just watched the world burn down and couldn't understand why.

Then he blinked.

The cigarette jerked on his lips. He inhaled, deep and ragged. Smoke leaked from his nose like steam from a broken pipe. And when he looked up again, he was gone.

Or maybe what had been Ryan was gone, and something else was standing there.

His face twisted.

The rifle jerked upward.

"We got unfinished business," he growled, voice thick and hoarse.

"What the hell are you talking about?" Nate snapped—but then stopped.

Because Ryan was staring at him now with a new kind of intensity. Not anger. Not grief.

Madness.

There was something behind his eyes that didn't fit anymore. A flicker. A hitch. A twitch in the corners of his face like static crawling under skin.

Nate took a step back. Slowly.

Ryan stepped forward.

"I've been thinking. Watching you," Ryan said, pacing now, slow and uneven. "You, Nate... you're a coward. That's what you are. A plain, gutless coward."

He advanced.

Nate backed away.

"You're not your father, Nate. You're not even your brother."

His voice broke into ragged pieces.

"You're not a hunter. Never were. You're a victim. That's your place. That's your role."

"That's enough," Nate growled. He raised his own rifle, hands tight. He took a breath, slow and measured, trying to anchor them both. "Put the damn thing down. Just... put it down. You hear me?"

Ryan's laugh was sharp and dry, like something breaking. "Look at you. Hands shaking. You gonna black out again like when that thing came for me? You froze, Nate. You just watched."

"Ryan, listen to me—"

"No, you listen." His voice flared. "You still don't get it! You never did! This place—this forest, Jesse, the old man—it was ours! We bled for it. We remembered. And you? You just came back like nothing happened. You woke it up."

Spit flew from his lips.

"It killed everyone but you. Not you."

His hands shook harder now, but the barrel never wavered.

"And you think you're just gonna walk away? Just go back to your little life like none of this ever happened?"

Nate's fingers clenched tighter around the rifle, anger bubbling up like acid through his chest.

"Jesus, Ryan," he snapped. "Do you even hear yourself right now?"

But Ryan kept coming. One step. Then another. The rifle twitching in his hands, a snake ready to strike.

His eyes were lit from within. Not with clarity—but with conviction.

With obsession.

"This is justice, Nate," he said, voice rough as gravel.

"It took everyone. You don't get to be the one who walks away. This is how it ends. You came back—so you stay. The forest wants you."

He paused.

And then, in a voice so calm it was terrifying:

"And maybe…"

A smile twisted its way across his face.

"…so do I."

Nate's breath caught in his throat. The weight of it all—the forest, the blood, Jesse's name carved in silence—threatened to crush him.

"You're insane," he said, stepping back again. His voice shook, but only with fury. "You're a goddamn psychopath."

His grip on the rifle tightened.

"You think this is justice?" His voice rose. "You woke it up, Ryan. You! You killed that boar—the real one—the wounded one. And you didn't just kill it… you sat in its blood like it meant something to you. Like you enjoyed it."

Ryan's head tilted slightly, eyes narrowing, listening.

"You were always like this," Nate spat. "Always on edge. Always one kill away from losing it. This thing? This creature? It came for you. Because of you. And now everyone's dead."

His voice cracked.

"Because of you, goddamn it!"

Ryan didn't stop.

He stepped forward again—measured, deliberate.

A sharp, guttural sound dragged from deep within his throat.

A low, deliberate grunt.

"So. You're staying right here," Ryan growled.

"Then we'll see what came for who."

His eyes narrowed, twitching at the corners. The grunt that followed didn't sound forced—it came like instinct. Like it had always been part of him, waiting.

Something changed in his face. Not rage—something wilder. Feral.

It shimmered behind his eyes, in the way he hunched, less man than beast now—something low, heavy, and full of teeth.

They circled, rifles raised, boots sinking into moss. A slow orbit, tense as wire.

Nate could barely breathe.

But it wasn't fear—not exactly.

It was hotter. Sharper.

Rage.

Unwanted, but rising all the same.

And what scared him most wasn't Ryan.

It was himself.

What he might become.

"I thought about busting your face the second I saw you," Ryan muttered, almost conversational. His voice was low and flat—too calm. "Felt it in my gut. Like an itch I couldn't scratch."

He smirked, then let out another of those strange, guttural grunts—half amusement, half threat.

"I even got my chance, remember?" Ryan sneered. "Would've gone harder if it hadn't been for…"

He jerked his head toward his torn-up shoulder, the bandage already dark and crusted, then gave a lopsided, mocking shrug—casual, like the pain was just background noise now. The rifle in his hands twitched, barely controlled.

"But I don't want that anymore," he said softly, the edge in his voice like a blade drawn slow.

"No.

Not now."

His grin widened.

"I leave you here—with your furry friend. Let him rip you apart. That's justice, Nate. That's balance."

Nate's jaw clenched.

"Ryan," he said, voice iron-flat. "This is your last chance. We can still get out of here. Sit down. Drive away. We don't have to do this."

His knuckles went white around the rifle.

"Or…"

Nate's voice was tight, every word like a pulled trigger.

"I swear to God—I will shoot you."

Ryan let out a high, brittle laugh.

"Oh yeah? That supposed to scare me?"

He took a step forward and shoved the barrel of his rifle into Nate's chest.

"Do it then. Let's see who pulls the trigger first."

Nate's hands trembled.

But he held.

His breath was ragged, vision narrowing around Ryan's twitching eye, the way his finger ghosted over the trigger.

And then—

Movement.

A twitch in Ryan's hand. A narrowing of his gaze.

He was going to fire.

Nate saw it—too clearly.

And in that instant, the world cracked open.

The memory didn't drift in like a dream. It crashed—sudden and merciless. Like drowning.

He was a boy again.

The trees loomed, impossibly tall, towering like ancient guardians. The air was thick with the scent of pine sap and woodsmoke. Laughter rippled nearby— his father's voice, deep and easy, Jesse's younger, brighter. Someone was flipping meat on the grill. Smoke coiled lazily through the branches, curling like a ghost into the sky.

No one was watching him.

And that was when it happened.

His small hands reached for the old rifle.

Too heavy. Too long. The stock awkward against his shoulder. His fingers trembled—just like they did now.

Still, he aimed.

And pulled the trigger.

A crack like lightning splitting bark.

A scream—raw and real.

The man dropped—fast and heavy, like something cut loose from the world.

Blood burst across his chest, sudden and violent, blooming like spilled paint.

Everything turned red.

It spread quickly—down his shirt, into the grass, across the dirt. A widening stain. A silent scream.

Voices rose in shock.

Yells.

Racing footsteps.

Chaos breaking loose.

All eyes turned to him.

To the boy.

To Nate.

Frozen, small, and shaking, with the echo of the shot still ringing in his ears.

The rifle slipped from Nate's hands as he stumbled backward, sobbing.

Not understanding.

Not really.

And then—

Jesse's voice.

Soft, almost tender, threaded through the memory like breath:

"You'd rather wallow in your own damn misery. Drown in it. Maybe it's safer for you that way. Staying broken means you never have to move forward…"

…to move forward…

Something clicked.

Inside him.

A fracture snapped back into place—not with peace, but with decision.

Nate blinked.

Ryan was still there, leering.

The grin. The challenge.

And suddenly, Nate didn't feel fear.

He felt clarity.

His hands stopped shaking.

The guilt, the weight, the memory—it was still there, but it didn't own him anymore.

He squeezed the trigger.

His eyes shut tight, bracing for the sound, the recoil, the death—

Click.

Nothing.

Just a hollow, empty sound.

No fire. *No bullet.*

Ryan's laughter exploded, manic and breathless.

"Oh man—you should've seen your face!"

He stepped in close, eyes gleaming with cruel delight.

"You really thought I wouldn't check? Idiot!"

The rifle swung.

Hard.

The butt of it cracked into Nate's nose with a sickening snap.

Pain detonated—blinding, white-hot, like lightning shattering through bone.

Blood surged up, hot and sudden, washing over his face, filling his mouth with copper.

He staggered—then dropped, the world tilting violently beneath him.

The ground rose to meet him: slick, unyielding, alive with mud, shattered twigs, and damp, rotting leaves.

He hit hard.

The impact stole the breath from his lungs.

Everything spun.

Light fractured into shards.

Stars bloomed behind his eyes, bright and cruel.

And then—only the thudding pulse in his skull and the taste of blood.

His hands slipped. His rifle gone.

Ryan's boots approached, slow and steady.

He was still laughing.

Standing over Nate now, the sun behind him like a twisted halo.

"I'm leaving," Ryan said, breathless. "Enjoy your stay, Nate."

He leaned in slightly, voice dropping to a venomous whisper.

"Say hi to your friend in the trees."

Nate didn't move.

Pain pulsed like thunder in his skull. The world narrowed, swam. Blood from his broken nose streamed past his lips. He could barely hear the words—just a low murmur lost inside the roar of his own heartbeat.

He lay there.

Breathing hard.

Not even trying to get up.

The sky above shimmered, blue and fractured.

Sunlight cut through the canopy in thin, pale blades.

Somewhere far off, a bird took flight.

And for a long moment, Nate didn't move at all.

Just stared up, through the blur, as the forest watched in silence.

Ryan bolted.

He lunged toward the SUV like a man possessed, boots tearing through the underbrush, hands fumbling for the door.

But the sound in Nate's head wouldn't stop. That awful pressure, a low-frequency hum, rising. Building. Until it wasn't just in his skull anymore.

It was in the ground.

A vibration. Faint at first, like something stirring beneath the soil. But it grew stronger, deeper, until he could feel it in his bones.

Nate lifted his head from the muck, one hand pressed to his shattered nose, the other pushing him upright. He blinked through blood and dirt, confused. The forest swayed. The trees rustled with something more than wind.

He braced a hand against a tree trunk, hauled himself into a crouch.

The earth was trembling.

It wasn't in his mind.

It was real.

And then, the boar came.

Not from the path. Not from the road.

From the trees.

A blur of shadow and muscle. A silent hammer of tusk and rage. It didn't charge so much as erupt—bursting from the dense green like it had always been there, waiting.

Even in daylight, it moved like darkness. A streak of black hate, rippling through the forest.

Ryan turned too late.

There was a sound—a grunt, maybe a shout—and then he was airborne, limbs flailing like a broken doll. A red arc followed, painting the air behind him. He hit the ground with a sound that made Nate flinch.

A scream cut through the woods.

Nate had heard it before.

That kind of scream only happened in this forest.

He pressed himself harder against the tree, breath caught, eyes wide. Every instinct told him to vanish. To disappear into bark and root and moss.

Ryan was still moving.

Somehow.

He crawled, a trail of gore smearing the ground behind him. Blood soaked the grass, thick and black-red, pooling fast. Something slick trailed from his body. Torn meat. A glint of bone.

He wasn't whole anymore.

But he was alive.

And he was trying to crawl.

Nate stared, frozen in horror.

Ryan's eyes—wild and feral—caught his. He was choking, gargling on blood, dragging himself forward with the stubborn panic of something that refused to die.

And then the boar struck again.

It moved so fast it was a whisper.

Another impact, another wet crunch.

This time, Nate saw it clearly—the massive tusks driving into Ryan's side, lifting him like meat on a skewer, tossing him effortlessly. His body sailed through the air and crumpled against a tree with a sickening, boneless thud.

He landed in a heap. Twisted. Wrong.

Ryan coughed. Choked. Screamed.

And the boar... stopped.

It stood over him. Not moving. Not striking.

Just watching.

Blood dripped from its tusks, steaming in the morning air.

Its black eyes shimmered with something that wasn't quite animal.

Ryan was dying. His breaths came in shallow, wet gasps. Blood spilled from his mouth, his nose. His hands clawed at the earth.

Then, one final shudder.

Stillness.

He was gone.

The boar tilted its head.

Toward Nate.

It didn't move.

It didn't need to.

It was waiting.

Nate didn't breathe. Didn't blink. The silence throbbed in his ears.

Slowly, as if the motion might save him, he began to crawl.

One inch at a time.

His hand grazed something cold and metal in the grass.

Ryan's rifle.

Fingers closed around it.

He pulled it toward him, muscles burning. His legs refused to work. He got to his knees, swaying.

The rifle was heavy. So much heavier than before.

It shook in his grasp.

But he raised it.

One breath.

Then another.

And he aimed.

The barrel pointed straight at the boar.

Its black eyes gleamed, catching the sunlight that filtered through the canopy— twin obsidian mirrors reflecting Nate's own trembling face.

And for one long, breathless moment, the world froze.

Their gazes locked.

Nate couldn't look away.

He swallowed, throat dry and tight.

Faces surged in his mind, flickering like dying flames.

Tyler—eyes wide and empty, glassy in death.

Jesse—so still, rain painting his face like mourning.

Dale—whispering, "It's here," right before the dark took him.

Ryan—screaming, torn apart.

So much blood.

So much death.

And somehow, he was still here.

Still breathing.

Nate didn't pull the trigger.

He didn't move.

Instead, he sank down, slow and hollow, until he was crouched again beside the tree.

He shifted back, just enough to lean against the rough bark, feeling the press of it through his shirt, grounding him, holding him upright.

The rifle lowered to his lap. His hands wouldn't stop shaking.

Blood pooled beside him, warm and sticky. The metallic scent filled his nose.

His ears rang with static.

He wasn't sure if he was crying.

Across the clearing, the boar still watched him.

It didn't advance.

Didn't retreat.

Didn't even blink.

It just watched.

And Nate watched back.

His heart pounded—a drumbeat of helplessness and defiance. This wasn't salvation. It wasn't punishment. It was something older. Something elemental.

Nate stared back—unblinking, unyielding.

He didn't look away.

His heart thundered in his chest, wild and frantic.

There was no plan. No miracle. No escape.

Only the forest.

Only the eyes staring into him like pits of night.

Death looked at him.

Not as a stranger, but as something inevitable.

A reckoning, born from too much blood spilled beneath these trees.

His breath caught, then steadied.

Nate raised the rifle again. Hands still shaking. Grip firm.

Not in defiance. Not in fear.

But because it was all he had left.

And as the sunlight spilled across the blood-soaked earth,

the forest whispered not of mercy—

but of memory.

Chapter 10:

To Be Prey

The forest did not speak.

It only watched.

Branches sagged low with mist, trees bowed in silence as if in mourning. The morning air hung damp and metallic, and though it cut like glass, Nate didn't feel it anymore. His coat was half-open, streaked with blood—his own—still seeping in thin rivulets from his shattered nose and split brow. He no longer bothered to wipe it away. It trailed over his lips, down his neck, soaking into his collar. Meaningless now.

Pain. It radiated through every limb, every nerve ending—a chorus of agony that echoed the blows Ryan had dealt him, the brutal fall, the bone-deep ache of everything breaking down. And yet, it was the only thing left to tether him to reality. Pain, cruel as it was, still meant he was alive.

One shoulder hung lower than the other, the joint likely torn. His left arm trembled without rhythm, jerking in small, useless spasms. He couldn't say if it was fear, shock, or simply that something vital inside him had finally broken loose. His breath came in ragged gasps, and with every inhale, it felt like the forest was climbing deeper inside him—through his throat, into his lungs, rooting itself there.

And yet, through all of that—only one thought survived.

Alone.

Not just a condition. Not a status. A presence. A thing that wrapped around him like smoke and bone. The word echoed in his skull, over and over, until it wasn't a word at all but a pulse.

Alone.

Truly, finally, absolutely alone.

The thought didn't just weigh him down—it folded in around him. Coiled cold tendrils through his chest, into the hollow behind his ribs, like smoke that froze instead of burned. His teeth began to chatter, not from the cold, but from the pressure of knowing no one would ever speak his name again.

There was no more Ryan.

No Dale.

No Tyler.

No Jesse.

Only the trail of broken earth, the memory of screams now fading into the soil, and the forest that refused to forget.

Nate's gaze flicked—not to the monster that stood ahead, but just slightly to the side.

There, splattered like grotesque paint across the ferns and roots, lay what was left of Ryan.

It didn't resemble a man anymore. Red. Torn. Pieces. A wet carpet of flesh and shattered bone.

Nate swallowed hard. The taste of blood filled his mouth.

So this, then. This was *the end.*

This is what would become of him.

He inhaled, slow and deep, like someone savoring their final breath.

Then he moved.

His legs resisted, but he forced them to obey. He rose—if it could be called that—and limped forward, the rifle clenched in his right hand like a talisman. His fingers twitched around the stock, numb from cold or terror or exhaustion—he couldn't tell. Maybe it didn't matter.

The mud sucked at his boots, every step an effort. Branches scraped at his arms like fingers, like claws, as if the forest itself was trying to pull him back.

He stepped carefully.

Deliberately.

The boar stood ahead, a statue of muscle and shadow, and its eyes tracked his every move. Unblinking. Unwavering. Not aggressive—yet—but focused. Possessive.

Like it already owned him.

Nate's heart pounded, not fast, but deep. Heavy. Like a funeral drum.

He didn't dare look away now. But still—his eyes slid once more to the bloodstained ruin that used to be Ryan.

A chill swept through him, deeper than any wind. He took another breath. And another.

Then another step.

The forest said nothing.

But it watched.

The Boar stood in a shallow clearing—a living wall of muscle and bristled hide, its hide scarred with the stories of a hundred years, its tusks slick with blood not yet dry. Flies buzzed around the steaming viscera at its feet, but the beast paid no mind.

It didn't rush. And Nate knew why.

There was no escape from here.

This wasn't a fight. This wasn't a chase. This was the final moment in a trap too vast to see until it closed. The forest itself was the snare, the trees the bars of the cage, and this monster the will that ruled it.

Nate could hear it breathing—deep, guttural huffs that steamed in the air like smoke from a furnace. Yet it stood at a distance. Its nostrils flared. Its eyes burned, low and terrible, like coals buried deep in ash, watching him with something older than thought. Patience. Judgment.

His knees buckled, but he did not fall.

He raised the rifle with both hands, aiming at the center of that monstrous chest. Every nerve screamed. But thinking had already fled him. There were no tactics left. No plans. No escape. He didn't know how to win, didn't even know what the creature wanted—if it wanted anything at all.

His mind, starved and reeling, offered nothing. Maybe it was the pain, maybe the exhaustion, or maybe it was just that his brain had run dry.

Nate sniffed hard, blood dribbling down his lips. He squinted, steadying the rifle as best he could. Just one more shot. One more act.

He pulled the trigger.

The crack of the shot tore across the trees, echoing like a scream through the cold air.

The boar flinched. Barely.

Like a man brushing away a gnat. Or even less.

And in its eyes—there was something. Not rage. Not fear. Something deeper. A flicker of… recognition? Or disdain. Its gaze gleamed from within, and the world around Nate shifted.

Something changed.

Not in the boar.

In everything else.

A tremor passed beneath his boots. Not imagined—he could feel it. Like a low drumbeat in the bones of the earth. The trees stirred, but not with wind— branches swayed in separate directions, wind gusting from nowhere, spinning chaotically around him. The hum returned, a vibration deep in the roots. The forest shook.

Still, the boar did not charge.

It moved.

Slowly. Gracefully.

One hoof after another sank into the earth with dreadful calm. Not rushing. Not lunging. Simply claiming what it already owned.

Nate fired again.

His hands trembled so hard he nearly dropped the rifle. The shot cracked, but he barely saw where it landed.

Blood sprayed from the beast's shoulder—but not red.

It was black. Thick. Like tar.

And it didn't stop.

The boar let out a sound—low, grinding, like a millstone tearing bone. The very air trembled.

Then it sped up.

Its muscles rippled. Hooves sparked. It surged forward.

Not alone.

Nate heard it—the thundering of hooves, not one but many, all around him. The sound came from everywhere—like the forest itself had a hundred legs and all of them were running.

He spun in place, eyes wide, searching the trees. Nothing. Nothing but sound. But it felt like the whole world was collapsing inward.

He staggered back.

Then it came.

The charge was faster than thought. Faster than breath.

Nate tried to run. Turn. Move.

But the forest closed around him. Trees blurred. The ground twisted beneath him.

He was *too slow.*

Everything slowed to nightmare speed. His feet dragged like they were in tar. The world stretched. Time bent.

He saw the boar now—not as a shape but as a force.

He felt the tusks before he saw them.

They tore into him like scythes, cold and merciless.

Pain exploded through his ribs—sharp, electric, all-consuming. It wasn't pain like he'd known before. It didn't sit in one place. It raced like fire, like lightning through nerve and bone, turning muscle to liquid. His scream died before it ever reached his throat. All he could do was feel.

Nate was airborne.

He felt the sick lift of gravity's betrayal as something—tusks, fury, the sheer will of the forest—launched him into the air. He was weightless for a breathless second.

Then the world flipped. *Crashed. Screamed.*

He hit the ground with a sickening crunch. Something inside cracked—no, shattered—and he knew with a hollow certainty: that sound had come from him. From his own breaking.

Blood sprayed across the dead leaves like rain.

He curled inward, instinct taking over. Hands clutched at his ribs, but it was too late for defense. His side blazed with white-hot agony. Bones out of place. Muscles torn. Something inside twisted wrong, grinding when it shouldn't move.

He gasped for air—but there was none.

Only the taste of metal. Blood. Panic.

His mouth opened wide, dragging at the air, but it wouldn't go in. Every breath was a struggle against a crushing weight inside his chest. As if the forest itself had taken hold of his lungs and refused to let them fill.

He moved a leg. Just barely. Felt it twitch.

Some small part of his brain registered this as good news.

He turned, inch by inch, the world tipping wildly. He couldn't see clearly anymore. Everything shimmered at the edges.

He crawled.

Slow. Staggered. Each movement came with a cost. Inches felt like miles. His body was no longer something he lived in—it was something he dragged behind him.

He didn't know where he was going. Didn't know why.

He just moved.

Somewhere behind him, a growl echoed through the trees. Or maybe beside him. Or in front. It was everywhere now. Like the forest had grown a thousand mouths, and all of them were snarling.

The ground vibrated again. Branches above swayed though no wind touched them. Roots curled in the soil like serpents.

His head pounded—each heartbeat like a hammer behind his eyes. A dull, bludgeoning pulse. His temples throbbed in rhythm with the chaos.

He clawed at the ground, blood-slick fingers sinking into mud. Moss smeared into open wounds. Earth filled his nails.

Then—

A glint of metal.

Distant. Gleaming.

The truck.

There it was. Through the branches, tilted and half-sunken in the slope, but there.

Hope.

Or maybe a cruel joke.

Nate reached out a hand, fingers trembling, hovering just above the earth. He paused.

Too far.

The pain screamed in protest as he dragged himself forward again, sobs tearing through his throat—not from grief or fear, but from the sheer effort it took to stay conscious.

He clenched his teeth.

And pulled.

Nails tore. Muscles burned. Blood smeared behind him like a trail of ruin.

But still, he moved.

The forest did not go silent.

Another growl. Closer.

A shadow swept past. Black and massive and impossibly fast.

The boar.

It moved again.

He heard the snort. The grunt. The crash of hooves tearing across the roots.

This time, Nate saw it.

The tusks struck his thigh. Not a slash—an obliteration.

Pain, deeper than pain. A new kind. Raw, primal. It hit him in waves, lighting up his entire nervous system. He didn't even scream. He couldn't.

He flew again. A rag doll. A broken thing.

And then—*impact.*

The earth caught him like stone. All the air left his body. It felt like a house had collapsed on his chest.

The world spun. Colors bled into each other. Red. Green. Black.

Everything was too bright and too dim at once. He couldn't make sense of the sky or the ground or the shape of his own limbs.

He didn't move.

Couldn't move.

Blood soaked through his jeans, hot and thick. It pooled beneath him like a blanket of heat.

He rolled onto his back—not by decision, but from sheer inertia.

His chest heaved. Each breath scraped.

His eyes blinked wide, staring up.

The sky above was a dull smear of gray. Endless. Lifeless. The pines above him stretched like monuments, their branches waving in silence.

They looked like mourners.

A funeral of trees.

The wind picked up, rattling the limbs above. Leaves stirred like whispers.

He was still alive.

But only just.

He didn't move.

He couldn't.

His body was a collapsed cathedral, broken stone and splintered wood, each limb a ruined beam. The only part of him that still worked were his eyes—blinking, slow, sluggish. That was all he had left.

And then—

Breath.

Not his own.

A low, hissing breath steamed beside him, hot enough to warm the dirt. Nate felt it before he turned. The sound scraped against his ears like sandpaper.

The boar.

It was right there.

Towering.

Watching.

Its breath fogged the air between them, rising in slow, steady clouds. The heat of it burned the blood-caked skin on Nate's cheek.

It did not charge.

It waited.

Nate coughed—a wet, rasping sound. Blood painted his lips. His fingers dug weakly into the leaves and mud beside him, and somehow, against every rule of pain and broken bone, he pushed himself upright.

Every inch was agony.

His spine was a column of fire. His ribs shrieked with each breath. But he sat up, slowly, inch by trembling inch, and leaned his weight against the nearest tree. The bark pressed cold and unforgiving into his back.

He stared into the forest.

The boar still loomed over him.

Why am I still alive?

The question echoed in his head like a bell tolling at a funeral. *What does it want?*

The beast's eyes glowed like embers, like something that remembered fire. Its breath was loud, ragged, heavy—like a machine worked by rage alone.

Nate looked into those burning eyes.

He felt like a man kneeling at the gallows, staring into the executioner's face. The verdict had already been given. The noose was already around his neck.

He let his head slump back against the trunk, too tired to hold it up anymore.

"Goddamn it," he rasped, the words slurred through cracked lips and blood. "What are you waiting for?"

Silence.

Just breath. And eyes.

And then—

The past came screaming.

Not memories. Shrapnel. Shards. Like glass. Like teeth.

They spun around him, wrapped tight like wire around his throat. They didn't ask permission. They didn't wait.

A boy. A clearing. A gun.

A shout. A fall.

Blood.

Hands trembling. A chest that wouldn't rise.

His brother's voice, years later:

«It wasn't your fault. You didn't know. Let it go, Nate. Please. Let it go.»

Tyler's whisper by firelight:

«If you saw it... you're already dead.»

And then—

His father.

Rifle over one shoulder. Morning fog curling around his boots. Eyes hard, voice soft:

«You're not a hunter till you know what it feels like to be prey... Hunting's an honest game, son. You win, or you die. That's the deal.»

You're not a hunter...

...to be prey.

The words hit like a hammer.

Over and over.

Preyyyy.

It pulsed in his skull. Crawled under his skin. Echoed in his ribcage like something alive. His eyes flew open.

And the boar was still there.

Watching.

He stared back.

And something inside him clicked.

Like a puzzle that had always been missing its final piece—

and now, suddenly, it was there.

The shape of it. The fit. The truth.

Everything fell into place.

The weight in his chest didn't vanish—but it made sense now.

His eyes sparked with something new. Not defiance. Not fear.

Recognition.

His thoughts stopped spinning.

They folded inward, orderly, like pages closing on a chapter long overdue.

His mind, for the first time in what felt like years, was quiet.

His lips parted.

The breath that escaped was dry, ragged—full of dust and blood—

but it was steady.

Anchored.

Real.

«I get it now,» he whispered.

«I know what I am. This... this was never about killing you. It was about seeing you. Facing it. Facing myself.»

His eyes burned. From pain. From understanding.

A beat passed.

Then another.

And slowly—trembling, dragging—he reached across his body.

His fingers brushed the rifle.

Still strapped to him. He worked the clasp with failing hands. It took too long. His limbs barely responded. When the strap finally came loose, the weapon dropped into his lap like dead weight.

He stared at it.

Then he pushed it away.

Weakly. Almost lazily.

The rifle thumped into the dirt.

No echo. No sound. Just the hush of the trees.

Nate looked forward.

Breathed in. Slow. Shallow. Accepting.

"If I can't make sense of this," he said quietly, "maybe I don't deserve to walk out."

A pause.

His voice cracked.

«You're not a beast. You're a mirror. A reckoning.»

His fingers curled again into the soil.

«But if I'm wrong—kill me already. I don't care anymore. You hear me? I don't—»

He met the boar's gaze.

Fully.

Unflinching.

A man at the end of something.

Not begging.

Just done.

The boar didn't move.

Not at first.

It stood there for what felt like an eternity, eyes locked with Nate's, glowing with something deeper than fire. The stare passed through him—not at him, not around him. Through him. It peeled back the skin of his soul, read the truths beneath the lies, the memories beneath the blood.

It wasn't a stare you could fool.

What the beast saw wasn't rage. It wasn't hate.

It was memory.

Old.

Older than men. Older than the pines. Older than bones and teeth and stories whispered in smoke. It was the weight of time. The gravity of knowing. Something so ancient it didn't need words to exist.

The boar snorted, drawing in a breath—slow, deliberate—as if scenting more than blood. As if reading the shape of Nate's fear, his pain, his surrender. The moment held, motionless. Timeless.

Then, with a grace that didn't match its weight, it stepped forward.

Its snout lowered.

It pressed, just slightly, into Nate's chest. A nudge—not soft, not violent. Just... real.

A gesture. A mark.

Recognition.

And then the beast turned.

And walked past him.

Into the trees.

Back into the mist and root and shadow.

Its hooves, impossibly, made barely a sound. Each step was measured, deliberate. The mist parted around it like curtains drawn aside. Trees swayed as it passed, bending—not from wind, but as if in deference.

And then it was gone.

Swallowed.

Silence.

Nate didn't move.

He waited, frozen in disbelief. For the pain. For the end. For the final scream that would tear him apart. For death to come back and finish what it started.

But nothing came.

It felt like a joke. Like a mercy he hadn't earned.

For the first time in what felt like days—

There was no pain.

Only quiet.

Only breath.

Only him.

He waited. Still expecting the claws. The hooves. The tusks. But it never came.

Is it over?

He blinked. Turned his head.

And there it was.

The bloodstain. Where Ryan had been.

A carpet of red, already drying in the dirt.

Nate's stomach turned, but nothing rose. Just silence in reply. Just the taste of iron and ash on his tongue.

Then—

A glint.

Sunlight on glass.

The truck.

The windshield caught the rising light and bounced it back into Nate's eyes. Bright. Sharp. Real.

He moved.

Slow. Like ice cracking. His limbs didn't obey so much as drag themselves forward, muscle by trembling muscle.

He gripped the tree beside him and pushed. His knees almost gave, but somehow—they didn't. His legs held.

He stumbled forward.

The world around him shimmered, unreal. Like walking through a dream, or the surface of deep water. Everything swam in mist. Every sound echoed too long or didn't echo at all.

The pain came back in a wave.

It buckled him.

He doubled over, mouth open in a voiceless scream, gripping a tree so hard the bark bit into his skin. When the pain ebbed, he forced himself upright again.

One step.

Then another.

Each one a war.

He reached the truck.

His hand shook as it grasped the door. It took two tries to open it. When it finally swung wide, he collapsed into the seat like a man falling through space.

Blood smeared across the wheel. His breath fogged the cracked windshield.

He turned the key.

The engine roared.

His hands dropped from the wheel for a moment, trembling, bloodied. The sound of the engine felt distant, like it was happening to someone else. His vision blurred—just for a second—but he blinked it back. He didn't feel his ribs anymore, not really. Just the pull of motion. Of forward. Not thinking.

Just... driving.

Nate just sat there for a long moment.

Staring.

The forest outside. The forest behind. The thing that almost ended him, the memories that had.

Something had changed.

Not just around him.

Inside.

He didn't feel fear anymore.

The ache in his bones was unbearable, but his soul—

His soul was light. Like something had been left behind in those woods. Something he no longer needed. A weight he'd carried so long, he didn't realize what it was until it was gone.

And something else had been found in its place.

Not strength.

Not peace.

Something deeper.

Clarity.

He wasn't whole. But he was real.

He reached for the gear.

His fingers, bloody and shaking, wrapped around it.

His eyes lit with something that hadn't been there before.

And he hit the gas.

Hard.

The tires screamed against the dirt. The truck lurched forward, tearing through the mist, carving a path away from the trees.

The sun crested the ridge.

Light spilled across the broken mountain road like gold dust shaken from a god's hand. The sky opened wide above him—blue, vast, endless. The kind of blue that didn't seem real. The kind that felt like forgiveness.

Behind him, the forest shrank into the distance.

Tall. Dark. Watching.

Not chasing.

Not gone.

But still.

In the rearview mirror, something shifted.

A flicker. A breath of shadow between two trees.

Then nothing.

Gone.

But not forgotten.

Nate's chest rose.

Fell.

Rose again.

He glanced at the mirror—not at the woods, but at himself.

His face was torn, bruised, split open in three places.

Dried blood streaked his temple.

His lips were cracked.

His nose—broken and bloodied—sat crooked across his face, swollen and dark.

But in his eyes, there was something new.

Not pain. Not fear.

Clarity.

Fire.

A man who had faced something vast and terrible—and walked away different.

Not relief.

Not triumph.

Something deeper.

He had walked into that forest carrying a gun and a grudge.

He left it carrying nothing.

And yet—somehow—**more than ever.**

The forest doesn't forget.

But sometimes… it lets you live.

He pressed harder on the gas.

The engine rumbled, eager.

The road ahead shimmered in the morning light like a promise.

He didn't look back.

Not again.

Not ever.

The forest had taken enough. He left what it wanted—and kept only what mattered.

The trees behind him blurred into distance.

The road rose to meet the sun.

And Nate drove on.

THE END

Leave the review

If you enjoyed this book, I'd really appreciate it if you left your honest feedback. I love hearing from my readers and I personally read every single review.

Thank you for your purchase!

Printed in Dunstable, United Kingdom